VOL

27
Eddie and the Fire Engine

Carolyn Haywood
AR B.L.: 4.2
Points: 3.0   MG

Eddie and the Fire Engine

Betsy saw Mr. Ward driving his fire engine very slowly up to the entrance of the Town Hall. On the seat beside Mr. Ward, leaning against him, was the funny little Santa Claus Mr. Ward had made. When Mr. Ward stood up, Santa Claus toppled right over in a heap and everyone laughed. Then Mr. Ward picked up Santa Claus and handed him down to Mr. Wilson who tucked him under his arm and carried him up the steps of the Town Hall. There he deposited him on the wide brick wall and propped him up against a post. Santa Claus doubled up like a jackknife.

"Now see here, Santa Claus," said Mr. Wilson, "this is Christmas Eve and you have work to do. You'll have to come to life.

Very slowly Santa Claus began to straighten up. He stretched one arm out and then the other. Then he began to get up, and suddenly there was a lively little Santa Claus standing on his feet and calling out. "Merry Christmas! Merry Christmas! Step right up, boys and girls, and get your presents!"

"Why," shouted Betsy, "it's little Eddie! It's little Eddie!"

Eddie and the Fire Engine

Written by Carolyn Haywood
Illustrated by Betsy Lewin

BEECH TREE BOOKS, NEW YORK

To My Two Elisabeths
(Spelled with an S)
Who Dote on Little Eddie

Printed in the U.S.A.
First Beech Tree edition, 1992.
1 3 5 7 8 6 4 2

Library of Congress Cataloging-in-Publication Data

Haywood, Carolyn, 1898-1990
Eddie and the fire engine / written by Carolyn Haywood; illustrated
by Betsy Lewin.   p.   cm.
Summary: Eight-year-old Eddie Wilson, who collects vauable
property and stray animals, acquires a goat and an old fire engine.
ISBN 0-688-11498-9 :
[1. Fire engines—Fiction.]   I. Title.   PZ7.H31496Ed   1992
[Fic]—dc20   92-10403   CIP   AC

Contents

Chapter One

What the Weather Man Did to Eddie

Little Eddie Wilson pressed his nose against the windowpane and watched the raindrops bouncing in the street. They had been bouncing for days. Now it was Saturday and the weather man had said that it would be clear.

Papa was always saying "My friend the weather man says," but no matter what the weather man said it just rained and rained. And this was a special Saturday, a very special Saturday. It was Eddie's birthday and it was the day for the September Fair, and anyone who did not know how important the September

Fair was just did not know anything.

The September Fair was held every fall to raise money for charity. As long as Eddie could remember he had gone with Mother or his older brothers to the September Fair. When he was very little, he didn't know what it was all about. Then it was just a lot of balloons and pink sugar candy that looked like a wad of pink cotton to Eddie, and he loved balloons and pink cotton candy so he loved the September Fair. Now that Eddie was older, he understood more about the Fair.

He had said to his mother one day, "Mother, who is Charity?"

"Charity, dear?" said his mother. "Charity who?"

"Not Charity who," replied Eddie. "Who is Charity?"

"I haven't the slightest idea what you're talking about," said Mother.

"Why, I heard you say that the September Fair was for Charity," said Eddie. "What I want to know is, who is Charity?"

"Oh!" said Mrs. Wilson. "Charity isn't someone, Eddie. When we say that the Fair is for Charity, we mean that all of the money that is made is given to pay for the care of poor people in hospitals and children in day nurseries and to help the Red Cross and the Salvation Army."

Eddie's face shone. "Say! That's great!" he cried. "Do you think they would give me some money to take care of cats and dogs?" Eddie was always bringing stray cats and dogs home with him.

"Of course not," said his mother. "And remember, Father told you not to bring any more cats or dogs home."

"I haven't a single one," said Eddie. "Not a single cat or dog." And he had said it in a very sorrowful voice.

Eddie's breath clouded the windowpane as he pressed his nose against it, and he wrote his name with his forefinger over and over again and watched the rain run down the outside of the glass.

He heard his mother's footsteps in the hall, so he quickly took out his handkerchief and began to polish the window. "I'm cleaning the window for you, Mama," he called out as she came into the room. "If it wasn't raining so hard, I'd do the outside too."

"That's nice of you, Eddie," said his mother. "I'll get the chamois for you and you won't have to use your handkerchief, and you can do the inside of all of the windows."

Before Eddie could catch his breath, Mother was out of the room and in a moment she was back with the chamois and a little basin of water.

"It's wonderful to have such a thoughtful little boy," said Mrs. Wilson.

"Hum," said Eddie, as he wrung the water out of the chamois. "Uh—you want me to wash all of these windows?"

"Yes, darling," said Mother.

"All of these little panes of glass?" said Eddie in a worried tone of voice.

"Yes, darling," said Mother.

"In every window in the room?" said Eddie.

"Yes, darling," said Mother.

"Geepers!" said Eddie. "How did I get myself into this mess?"

"Why, Eddie," exclaimed his mother, "it was your idea to clean the windows. I didn't ask you to clean them."

Eddie looked at his mother with a puzzled expression on his face. The chamois hung from his hand. "It was?" he said. "Well, how did I ever happen to think of it?"

Eddie polished the windows while his mother sat in a chair, darning socks. Outside the rain puddles grew larger and larger.

"I'd like to give the weather man a poke in the nose," said Eddie.

"Why, Eddie Wilson!" exclaimed his mother. "It isn't the fault of the weather man that it's raining. The weather man isn't responsible for the weather."

"Well, he's responsible for my not having a birthday party," said Eddie.

"But, Eddie, you said you'd rather go to

the Fair than have a birthday party," said Mrs. Wilson.

"Sure," said Eddie, "but that was because I thought it was going to be a nice day and I was going to help Rudy at the fish pond and hang the packages on the fishing lines. If I'd known it was going to rain, I'd have had the party."

"You can still have the party," said Mother. "I can telephone your friends and invite them over."

"They wouldn't have time to buy any presents now," said Eddie.

"Eddie!" cried Mrs. Wilson. "I'm ashamed of you."

"Well, I take a present when I go to a birthday party," said Eddie. "You always say 'Don't forget to buy Betsy a birthday present.' Why am I supposed to forget all about my own?"

"Because that is being unselfish," said Mother.

"Well, I wish my birthday had been yesterday," said Eddie. "Then I'd have had a party at school and I could have been unselfish today.

But I had to go get born on Saturday and instead of having a birthday party or going to the Fair, I'm washing windows." Eddie dropped the chamois into the basin with a splash.

"You were not born on Saturday, darling," said Mother. "It just happens that your birthday falls on Saturday this year."

"Well, what does it fall on next year?" Eddie asked.

"Why, let me think," said Mother. "Why, on Sunday! Sunday, of course!"

"Oh!" groaned Eddie, throwing himself into a chair. "That's worse. Sunday! You won't let me have a party on Sunday."

"Never mind. We'll have it on Saturday," said Mother.

"O.K.," said Eddie, resuming his work on the windows.

"Oh, but that Saturday will be the September Fair," said Mrs. Wilson.

Eddie flung the chamois on the floor. "You mean I'll be in the same mess I am this year?"

"Pick up the chamois," said Mother. "And stop worrying about next year."

Just then Eddie's twin brothers, Joe and Frank, came into the house, the rain dripping from their raincoats. Joe and Frank were two years older than Eddie.

"There won't be any Fair today. It's postponed until next Saturday," said Joe.

"We've been over to the place," said Frank. "The carpenters have the booths built. They built them yesterday."

"'Cause the weather man said it was going to be clear today," said Joe.

"The weather man!" cried Eddie. "I hope he falls in a puddle and drowns."

"Eddie! Eddie!" cried Mrs. Wilson. "You must not speak that way. You must show respect for Father's friends."

Eddie turned from polishing the window and looked at his mother. His mouth was wide open. "You mean he really is a friend of Papa's?" he said.

"Of course he is," replied his mother.

"Haven't you heard Father say 'My friend the weather man'?"

"Sure I have," replied Eddie. "But I always thought he was fooling."

"Not at all," said Mother. "Father often has lunch with the weather man."

"What's his name?" asked Joe.

Mother thought for a few moments and then she said, "I don't seem to remember. I think it's something like Waters. No, I believe it's Showers."

"Showers!" cried the three boys in chorus.

"No wonder it rains all the time," shouted Eddie.

Mother laughed and went into the kitchen.

"You should see the swell stuff they have for the fish pond at the Fair," said Joe.

"They're going to call it the White Elephant Fish Pond," said Frank.

"You mean they're going to have white elephants swimming in it?" Eddie said with a twinkle in his eye.

"Of course not!" said Rudy, the oldest of the

Wilson boys, as he came into the room. "White elephants are all kinds of things that people give away because they're tired of having them around."

"You mean junk?" said Eddie.

"Oh, no. Not that bad," said Rudy.

"Oh!" cried Eddie, his eyes dancing. "You mean like valuable property?" Eddie was a great collector of things that the family called junk but that he called his valuable property. His private corner of the cellar was filled with Eddie's valuable property.

"Well, sort of, I guess," said Rudy.

"Gee!" said Eddie. "Maybe I can get some more stuff. I sure am glad you and I have the job of hanging the white elephants on the fishing lines."

"You can't keep them," said Rudy. "The people gave them so they could be sold to make money."

"Well, maybe I can buy some," said Eddie.

"It's fifty cents a catch," said Rudy.

Eddie's face grew long. "Well," he said,

"maybe I can buy one."

"You haven't got fifty cents," said Rudy. "You spent all your money last week for Billy Porter's birthday present."

Eddie let out a howl and flung the chamois at his oldest brother. It draped itself over Rudy's head and dangled from his ear. This made the twins shout with laughter. But Eddie was not laughing, for now he had been reminded of his own birthday and how the weather had spoiled it—no party, no Fair.

Mrs. Wilson came into the room to see what all the noise was about.

"He hit me with the chamois," said Rudy, peeling the wet chamois off of his ear.

"Well, he reminded me that I spent all my money on Billy Porter's birthday present," wailed Eddie. "I don't have any birthday presents, I don't have any money, and I have to wait until next Saturday to go to the Fair."

Mrs. Wilson handed Eddie the chamois. "Finish the windows," she said. "I'll give you fifty cents for washing the windows. You do them so nicely, Eddie. So quietly and without any fuss."

Eddie knew that his mother was poking fun at him. He tried not to smile as he went to work again on the windows.

"Will you give me fifty cents if I clean the outsides when it stops raining?" said Rudy.

"Nothing doing," cried Eddie. "I'm going to do the outside of the windows for fifty cents. Isn't that right, Mother? It was all my idea, wasn't it, Mother?"

"That's right," replied Mother. "It was all Eddie's idea to wash the windows."

At dinner that evening Eddie found a pile of packages at his place. With shining eyes, he opened them. There was a flashlight from Father, a pencil sharpener from Rudy, a game from Joe, a book about dogs from Frank, and a box of tricks from Mother. Eddie began to feel much more cheerful.

After the table had been cleared for dessert, Eddie watched the kitchen door to see what was coming in. Soon the door opened and in came

Rudy carrying a tray with plates of green ice cream on it. Pistachio was Eddie's favorite variety. Behind Rudy came Mother holding a big cake with lighted green candles. She placed it on the table in front of Eddie. The candles threw an orange light on his face as he bent over the cake to examine the decorations. It was covered with white icing and right in the center of the cake stood a little green umbrella. Streaks of chocolate icing were made to look like rain and below them, in green icing, were the words *Happy Birthday to Eddie! Sorry it rained.*

Eddie blew out all the candles with one terrific puff. Then he cut his cake and served a slice to each member of the family.

With a large mouthful of cake in his mouth, Eddie suddenly thought of something. "Oh, Papa," he mumbled, "what is the name of your friend the weather man?"

"The weather man?" said Father. "Why, Gus Sprinkler."

All the Wilson boys shrieked with laughter except Eddie. Mother was pounding little

Eddie on the back and there seemed to be a
great many cake crumbs flying around.

Chapter Two

The September Fair

The following Friday evening when Mr. Wilson came home from his office, Eddie ran to meet him.

"Hi, Papa!" he called out. "What does Mr. Sprinkler say about the weather?"

Father opened his newspaper and looked at the weather report. "Rain tonight and tomorrow," he read.

"Swell!" cried Eddie. "It'll be a nice day."

When Eddie woke up on Saturday morning the sun was shining brightly, although the grass was still wet for Mr. Sprinkler had been partly right. It had rained during the night.

Eddie dressed himself in a jiffy and bounded down the stairs.

"You had better hurry," said his mother, watching Eddie pour milk on his cereal. "The boys have been gone at least ten minutes, and I am going just the minute Father leaves. I have charge of the cakes and cookies and I mustn't be late."

"Oh boy! I'm glad I know you, Mama," said Eddie. "I can hardly wait to see the white elephants. They're over at Mrs. Porter's house and Billy Porter says there is some swell stuff. He says there's a fireman's hat and a fire bucket. He says it's the kind of hat the firemen used to have way back when Abraham Lincoln was a boy. He says the hat is higher than the ones they have now."

"Careful, Eddie," said Mrs. Wilson. "Stop waving that spoon around. You're getting corn flakes down the back of your collar."

Eddie put the spoon in the dish. "And Papa, he says the bucket is made of leather. Not a tin bucket, Mama, and not a wooden one, but leather. Billy says he wants that hat and bucket, but his father won't let him have them, not even if he bought 'em out of the fish pond. He says his father says it's just a lot of...uh...uh... Mama, can I have some more corn flakes?"

"What did Billy's father say, Eddie?" Mr. Wilson asked.

"Uh, there isn't any more milk in this pitcher," said Eddie, examining the pitcher carefully, as though he expected to find a little milk hidden in a corner.

"Turn it upside down, Eddie," said his father. "Maybe you'll find some milk stuck on the bottom. Then tell me what it was that Billy's father said."

"Excuse me, Papa, I have to get some more milk," said Eddie, as he slid off of his chair.

Eddie was a long time getting the milk. Meanwhile, Mr. Wilson said to Mrs. Wilson, "Billy Porter's father is a smart man. He doesn't have his house filled with things that other people have thrown away. I can see that old fireman's hat now. I can see it sitting on that chair and I can see the bucket. I'll probably fall over it the minute I come in the front door tonight."

Eddie came back, carrying the pitcher of milk. "I had to open a new bottle, Mama. This is nice milk. It's very nice milk, nice and white. I'll bet it was a nice cow they got this milk from. Do you think it was a Jersey cow or a Guernsey cow? Or maybe it was a Holstein cow. Holstein cows are awfully good cows. My teacher says that Holstein cows give very rich milk. Do you think this milk is a little grassy, Mama? It doesn't look grassy. No grass in it. My teacher says sometimes the cows eat too much garlic in the spring and then the milk tastes garlicky. I don't think this tastes garlicky, do you, Mama?" Here Eddie had to stop for breath.

Mr. Wilson rose to go. He kissed Mother good-by and stopped by Eddie's chair. He looked down at his youngest boy shoveling corn flakes into his mouth and said, "Eddie, I'll tell you what Billy Porter's father said. He said,

'It's just a lot of junk.' "

Eddie looked up at his father and grinned. "Yes, he did. But Papa, Mr. Porter doesn't know the difference between junk and valuable property. He isn't smart like you, Papa."

Mr. Wilson left the room, shaking his head.

Soon Eddie and his mother reached the Fair. It was being held on the grounds of a great big old house that stood in the center of ten acres of ground with lots of trees. It all looked very festive as Eddie and his mother drove in between the gate posts. The wooden booths were draped with bright-colored crepe paper, and all kinds of things were being put out on the counters.

Eddie could see Betsy's mother and another lady, Mrs. Jackson, arranging dolls in rows on one of the counters. Betsy was helping them. Betsy's little sister Star was playing with Lilly, whose mother, Mrs. Bell, worked for Mrs. Jackson and was the best cook for miles around.

Mrs. Bell was taking an enormous cake out of Mrs. Jackson's car. As Mrs. Wilson drove up, Mrs. Bell said, "Here you are, Mrs. Wilson. Here's the poundcake I promised I'd make for you."

"Oh, thank you so much, Mrs. Bell," Mrs. Wilson called. Then she said to Eddie, as he jumped out of the car, "I'm going to put the car in the barn."

"O.K.!" said Eddie, and he ran off to find the fish pond.

Soon he saw Rudy on the porch of the big house. "Rudy!" he called. "I'm here! Where are the white elephants?" Eddie ran up the porch steps. "Is this going to be the fish pond?"

"Yepper!" said Rudy. "You have to get under the porch, 'cause you're little, and hook the things on the line. The customers stand on the porch and hold the fishing rod so the line drops down over the side of the porch."

Eddie looked over the side of the porch and down into an enormous packing case. The front and sides were hidden by bushes. "Is this the fish pond?" he asked.

"Sure it is," said Rudy.

"Looks like a well to me," said Eddie.

"It's O.K.," said Rudy.

"Where are the white elephants?" Eddie asked.

"They're all under the porch," said Rudy.

Eddie was over the railing in a flash and under the porch. There he found a pile of packages of all sizes and shapes. They were wrapped in white paper.

"Hey, you can't tell what these things are," he called.

"Of course not," said Rudy. "You're not supposed to know what they are."

"You mean I'm not going to see all this valuable property?" Eddie wailed.

"It's to sell, Eddie," said Rudy. "It's to sell."

"But I want to see it," cried Eddie. "I want to see it."

"Listen," said Rudy. "Do you want to work here or shall I get somebody else?"

"I want to work here," said Eddie.

"Well then, get under there and pipe down."

Eddie crawled under the porch. There was a

large opening cut in the side of the packing case, and through this opening Eddie was to hook the packages on the fishing lines.

While he waited for the first customer, Eddie proceeded to feel all the packages. It was terrible to be surrounded with all these treasures and not know what they were. He wondered where the fireman's hat was and the bucket.

It did not take him long to locate the bucket. But where could the hat be? Eddie felt every package but not one felt like a hat. At last his face lit up. He picked up a package that was certainly a hatbox. This was it, of course. Someone had put the fireman's hat in a hatbox. Eddie set it aside carefully. He put it right on top of the bucket.

Just then Rudy called down, "Hey, Eddie! Are you ready? We're going to begin."

"Sure!" Eddie called back.

Eddie could hear feet trampling across the porch overhead. They were the customers. He heard Rudy say, "Where's your fifty cents?

Fifty cents for the White Elephant Fish Pond."

In a few minutes a line with a heavy hook on the end appeared in the opening of the packing box. Eddie reached out and hung a bulky package on the hook. It was drawn up slowly by someone overhead. Eddie could hear the paper being torn off and then shouts of laughter. Eddie thought it was terrible not to know what was going on, not to know what it was that had made everyone on the porch laugh.

"What did you get?" he shouted at the top of his lungs.

Betsy leaned over and called back, "Oh Eddie, you should see what I got!"

"It's no fun putting these things on if I can't see them," said Eddie.

"Well, I can get somebody else to do it," said Rudy. "There are plenty of kids up here who would be glad to do it. Do you want to come up?"

Eddie thought of the fireman's hat and the bucket. "No," he answered. "I'll do it."

"Well, get going then," said Rudy. "You're

keeping all the customers waiting. Put something on that line."

Again Eddie put a package on the hook and it was drawn up. Again he heard the paper being torn off, followed by shouts of laughter. But he didn't have time to ask what was in the package, for immediately another empty hook appeared in the opening. And no sooner had it been drawn up than another appeared.

Eddie was so busy he did not have a moment to rest.

By eleven o'clock all the white elephants were gone but two. Eddie stuck his head through the opening and shouted up to Rudy. "Hey, Rudy! I want to come up and fish. You come on down and let me fish. I got a dollar, you know, and you promised me I could fish twice. Come on down."

Rudy went down to Eddie. "How many have you got left?" he asked.

"Just two," said Eddie. "They're here."

"O.K.!" said Rudy. "Go on up and let the line down. Where's your dollar?"

Eddie handed his dollar to Rudy and went up on the porch.

Rudy looked at the hatbox and the other package that certainly looked like a bucket. "He sure saved himself the biggest ones," muttered Rudy. "I wonder what's in them."

When the hook appeared in the opening, Rudy hung the hatbox on it. Eddie lifted it up slowly and took it off. Then he let the line down again and pulled up the bucket. "That's all, folks," he cried. "That's all. Fish pond's closed. All sold out."

At that moment Mrs. Wilson appeared.

"Come, Eddie, we must have lunch right away. The twins are holding a table for us over in the Fair restaurant. Where's Rudy?"

"I'm coming, Mother," Rudy shouted from under the porch. "I'm starving."

"Come, Eddie," Mrs. Wilson repeated. "You can open those packages later."

"What shall I do with them?" Eddie asked.

"Put them in the back of the car," said his mother.

Eddie went off with his two packages to the car. After all, he knew what they were, so it was not so important to open them. It was dark in the barn, but he found the car and took the keys out of the dashboard. He unlocked the trunk and put the packages into the dark opening. Then he closed the lid and locked it again. He ran off to join his mother and the boys at the table in the restaurant. Mrs. Bell brought him a bowl of clam chowder.

The children were just finishing their lunch when the sound of a fire-engine bell rang out.

"There's a fire!" shouted Eddie.

"Let's go see!" cried Rudy.

The boys were on their feet. "Stay right here," said Mother. "It's the big surprise. It's the old fire engine. The firemen who are not on duty said they would bring it over and take the boys for rides. They have to turn it in next week because the new one has come."

"Geepers!" cried Eddie. "You mean I can go for a ride on it?"

"For ten cents," said Mother.

"Oh, Mama! Give me ten cents. Please give me ten cents so I can ride on the fire engine," pleaded Eddie.

Mrs. Wilson gave each of the boys ten cents and they ran off in the direction of the fire engine. It was already crowded with boys. Eddie hopped on and then he suddenly remembered his white elephants. They were just the thing.

"Will you wait a minute?" he shouted to the fireman who was driving. "Will you wait a minute? I gotta get something."

"O.K.!" said the fireman. "But be quick about it."

Eddie jumped down and flew to the car. He opened the trunk and felt for his treasures. He ripped the paper from the bucket. Then he tore the paper off the hatbox and raised the lid. He lifted the hat out by its rim and slapped it on his head. Then he grabbed his bucket and ran. The hat was so big it went right down over Eddie's ears and over his eyes. He pushed it up so that he could see where he was going and ran as fast as his legs would go toward the fire engine. The bucket swung beside him.

When he reached the fire engine, everyone was screaming with laughter. "Look at Eddie," they cried. "Hey, Eddie! Where did you get the hat?"

The fireman could hardly start the fire engine, he laughed so hard. He understood why Eddie wanted to get the fire bucket, but what he did not understand was why Eddie wanted to wear a high silk hat.

Chapter Three

The Fire Engine

Eddie climbed right up beside the driver of the fire engine and settled himself for the ride. His bucket swung from his arm.

"O.K.!" he said. "Let her rip!"

The fireman started the engine and they were off, with the twins, Joe and Frank, pulling the bell.

"What are you going to do with this fire engine?" Eddie shouted, loud enough to be heard above the noise of the bell and the yelling boys.

"Going to sell it to a secondhand car dealer,"

the fireman shouted back.

"Say! I wish my father was a secondhand car dealer," said Eddie. "That would be swell! I sure would like to have this fire engine. It's super!"

At this point Eddie took his hat off to look at it. He was a little surprised at its shape. It certainly did not look like any fireman's hat that he had ever seen before. But Billy Porter had said it was a fireman's hat, so it must be a fireman's hat, thought Eddie.

"Wasn't I lucky to get this hat?" said Eddie. "Billy Porter says this is the kind of hat the firemen wore when Abraham Lincoln was a boy."

"Well, that's news to me," said the fireman. "We used to call that a stovepipe hat."

Eddie laughed. "You did?" he said. "That's a funny name for a fireman's hat. But you get plenty of smoke, don't you?" Eddie thought this was very funny and he laughed so hard that his hat fell off into the street.

"Oh, there goes my hat!" he cried.

"Stop! My hat!" cried Eddie.

The fireman slowed down and drew up at the curb. Eddie climbed down and ran back for his hat, but there was no high-crowned hat anywhere around. There was a strange-looking black object lying in the street. It looked like a large black pancake. Eddie picked it up. It was his hat, but the crown was smashed as flat as though a steam roller had gone over it.

Eddie climbed back beside the fireman. "Look." he said. "You must have run over it."

"Let's have a look at that hat," said the fireman, taking it in his hand. And to Eddie's surprise, when the fireman took hold of the rim of the hat there was a noise almost as loud as a gunshot and there was the crown of the hat again, all stiff and as high as ever. Eddie could hardly believe his eyes.

"Eddie," said the fireman, "this isn't a fireman's hat. It's an opera hat."

The fire engine started off again.

"Well, I'll be jiggered!" said Eddie. "That's pretty neat, isn't it? Billy Porter didn't know what he was talking about when he said it was a fireman's hat, did he?"

"I think you got the wrong hat," said the fireman.

Eddie put the hat on again. Suddenly the fire engine went over a bump in the road and the hat folded up kerplunk and fell into the street.

"There goes my hat!" Eddie cried. "My hat!"

Once more the fireman brought the fire engine to a halt while Eddie picked up his hat. When he climbed back, the fireman said, "Now, that's the last time I'm going to stop for that hat. If it falls off again we leave it."

"O.K.!" said Eddie. "I'll hold it."

The fireman drove the fire engine all around the neighborhood, up one street and down another. The boys loved it. They had never had such a ride before.

In the meantime, the girls at the Fair were coaxing to be allowed to ride on the fire engine.

"I don't think it's fair," said Betsy. "It isn't fair not to let the girls ride."

"You'd fall off and get your pretty dress dirty," said Mr. Kilpatrick, the policeman.

"We could put on overalls," said Betsy. "It isn't fair."

"No, it isn't fair," said Lilly, who was standing beside Betsy and Star.

"'Tisn't fair," said Star.

"Well, I don't know what to do about it," said Mr. Kilpatrick. "The fireman said 'Only boys.'"

"Come on!" said Betsy, taking hold of Star's hand. "I have an idea. Come on!"

Betsy started for home. She went so fast that Star and Lilly had to run to keep up.

Just as the three reached Betsy's house, the fire engine went by. The boys waved and Eddie shouted, "Hi, Betsy! Hi!" The twins rang the bell. *Clang! Clang! Clang!*

In a few minutes the fire engine was back at the fair grounds and the boys jumped off.

As Eddie climbed down he said, "I'm going to see if I can get another dime and do it again."

"Well, don't lose your hat," the fireman

called, watching Eddie put his hat on.

Over by the ice-cream booth, Eddie saw his father. "Hello, Papa!" he called. "Papa, can I have a dime to ride on the fire engine? It's wonderful! Can I? I mean, may I?"

When Mr. Wilson saw Eddie, he burst out laughing. "Where did you get that hat?" he said.

"I got it out of the White Elephant Fish Pond," said Eddie. "But it's the wrong hat. I was supposed to get the fireman's hat. This is an opera hat." Just as Eddie said this, his hat collapsed again and fell off, rolling into the bushes.

Eddie dived under the bushes and scrambled around until he found his hat again. As he got up, he saw in the distance a boy wearing a fireman's hat. The boy was running toward the fire engine with two little boys running behind him.

Like a shot out of a gun, Eddie set out after them, but before he could catch up with them they were on the fire engine. Eddie was all out of breath, and just as he reached the fire engine it started on its second trip.

"Hey, you!" he shouted. "You've got my hat." But the boy paid no attention to him. Eddie couldn't tell who the boy was because the hat covered so much of his face.

There was nothing to do but sit down right where he was and wait for the fire engine to return. There his father found him. Mr. Wilson was carrying the fire bucket that Eddie had left beside the bushes when he set off after the boy wearing the fireman's hat.

"Papa," said Eddie, "the fellow with my fireman's hat just went off in the fire engine."

"Now, Eddie," said his father, "just because you wanted the hat, that doesn't make it yours. The boy got it out of the fish pond, so it's his."

"But it was a mistake!" said Eddie. "It was a mistake! I didn't mean to hang it on his fishing line."

"That doesn't make any difference," said his father. "The boy paid for it and it's his."

Eddie looked at the opera hat in his hand.

"Well," he said, "maybe he'll trade hats with me."

"I'll leave that to you," said Mr. Wilson.

"Could I have a dime, Papa, so I can have another ride on the fire engine when it comes back?" said Eddie.

Mr. Wilson put his hand in his pocket and took out a dime. He handed it to Eddie. "Here," he said, "and see that you're home in time for dinner."

"Thanks, Papa! Thanks!" said Eddie. "I won't be late for dinner."

Eddie waited for the fire engine. It seemed as though it would never return. Every once in a while Eddie could hear the *clang, clang, clang,* of the bell. It seemed to Eddie that the firemen were taking this crowd for a much longer ride. He did wish they would come back. Who could that fellow be with the fireman's hat, he wondered.

After what seemed an hour to Eddie, he heard the fire engine returning. He jumped up to watch it swing into the drive. He looked for the boy in the fireman's hat and soon he spied him. There he was, helping a little boy down. The little boy was wearing a riding cap that was much too big for him. Near by there was another little boy, and Eddie noticed that he had something on his head too. It looked like a man's cap with the visor hanging down in the back and resting on the little boy's shoulders.

Eddie rushed up to the biggest boy. "Hey!" he said. "Where did you get that fireman's hat?"

"In the fish pond," said the boy.

"Well, say, you know what? I'll trade you this hat," said Eddie, holding out the silk hat. "This is a wonderful hat. Here! Try it on."

With this, Eddie lifted the fireman's hat and to his amazement two long braids of hair, tied with red ribbons, fell out. Eddie saw that the boy was not a boy at all. It was Betsy.

"Hey, Betsy!" Eddie cried. "What's the big idea?"

"I had to get dressed up like a boy to get a ride on the fire engine," said Betsy.

"I'm a boy too," cried Lilly, pulling off the big cap.

"Me too," shouted Star, taking off the riding cap and letting her curls tumble out.

Eddie laughed. "Well, I'll be jiggered!" he shouted. "I didn't know you. But how about it, Betsy? Do you want to trade hats?"

"Oh sure, Eddie," said Betsy. "I'll trade hats with you."

"Thanks!" said Eddie. "That's great. You're a pal, Betsy."

Eddie put the fireman's hat on. "How do I look?" he said. "How do I look? Do I look like a real fireman?"

The hat hid Eddie almost completely, but Betsy said, "You look swell, Eddie. You look like a real fireman."

Eddie grabbed his fire bucket and ran to the fire engine, loading up for another trip. As he climbed up beside the driver, he called out, "I got the right hat this time."

"You sure have!" said the fireman. "But that stovepipe was a good hat."

"Do you really think so?" Eddie asked.

"Oh yes, it was a good hat," said the fireman.

Eddie sat quietly thinking for a moment. As the fireman put the fire engine into gear, Eddie said, "Yes, I guess that was a good hat. Well, I'll have to see what I can do about it."

When Eddie went home for his dinner, he carried his bucket into the house and set it by the front door. He put his wonderful hat on a chair.

As the family sat down to dinner, Mr. Wilson pointed to the hat on the chair. He looked at Mrs. Wilson. "Didn't I tell you?" he said.

"Yes," laughed Eddie's mother, "but you didn't fall over the bucket."

"Oh!" said Eddie's father. "Didn't I?"

Chapter Four

Eddie Goes to Dancing School

One day when Eddie came home from school his mother said, "Eddie, Mrs. Wallace was here this afternoon."

"You mean Toothless's mother?" Eddie asked.

"Eddie, that's a dreadful way to speak of Anna Patricia," said Mrs. Wilson.

"Well, it's true!" said Eddie. "She hasn't had any front teeth for such a long time that I guess she's never going to get any. And anyway, Anna Patricia is a silly name. Why don't they call her Anna or Patricia? Or just Pat? If I had a name like that I'd make everybody call me Pat."

"I guess Anna Patricia likes to be called by her full name," said Eddie's mother.

"Well, in school we all call her Toothless," said Eddie.

"Mrs. Wallace is forming a dancing class," said his mother. "She came to invite you to join."

Eddie looked at his mother with a face filled with horror. "A dancing class!" he cried. "What would I want to do that for?"

"Now, Eddie," said Mrs. Wilson, "it will be very nice for you to learn to dance. Dancing school is fun."

"Fun for the girls maybe, but not for boys. Are Rudy and the twins going?"

"It's just for the children in your room in school," said his mother.

"That's tough," said Eddie. Then his face brightened. "I know, Mama! You tell her Papa can't afford to send me to dancing school."

"But it's free, Eddie," said his mother. "Only

the girls have to pay."

"That's a mean trick," said Eddie. "And I bet I'll have to dance with Toothless. And she lisps!"

"Of course you'll dance with Anna Patricia," said Mrs. Wilson. "The dancing class is going to be held at her home."

Eddie sat down and held his head. "Ugh!" he said. "When?"

"Friday afternoon, at half past four," replied Mrs. Wilson.

"Friday afternoon!" wailed Eddie. "That's when we practice for the Saturday ball game."

"Eddie," said his mother, "you wouldn't want it to be on Saturday, would you?"

"Of course not," Eddie moaned. "But why does it have to be at all? Why do I have to learn to dance? Rudy and the twins don't have to learn to dance. Why do you pick on me?"

"Eddie, you will have a very nice time," said his mother. "Don't raise such a fuss. Go and see."

"If I don't like it can I stop?" Eddie asked.

"Yes, if you don't like it you can stop," his mother replied.

"O.K.!" said Eddie. "But don't tell Rudy and the twins that I have to go to dancing school."

"O.K.!" said Mrs. Wilson.

On Friday, when Eddie came home from school, his mother said, "Eddie, put on your best suit for dancing class."

"You mean my best Sunday suit?" said Eddie.

"Yes, dear," replied Mrs. Wilson.

"Golly! This dancing school business gets worse all the time," said Eddie.

Eddie washed his face and hands and soaked his hair with water. Then he took off his blue jeans and put on his best suit. "What will I do if I meet Rudy and the twins, all dressed up in my Sunday suit on Friday?" Eddie shrieked from his bedroom.

When he came downstairs his mother handed him a package. "These are your pumps, dear," she said.

"My what, Mama?" said Eddie, screwing up his nose.

"Your pumps," replied Mother, "your dancing pumps."

"What do I do with 'em?" Eddie asked.

"You wear them on your feet," said Mrs. Wilson.

"You mean I can't dance in my shoes?" Eddie cried.

"You would step on the little girls' feet, Eddie, in those clumsy shoes," said his mother.

"Serves 'em right!" said Eddie. "I'll walk all over Toothless's feet. Just let me at 'em."

"Eddie, do stop dawdling and get off," said his mother. "Have you money for bus fare? And don't forget to ask for a transfer."

Eddie pulled some change out of his pocket and looked at it. "O.K.," he said.

Just then he heard the twins coming in the front door. Eddie leaped like a deer and was out of the back door in a flash. He did not stop running until he reached his bus stop.

When the bus arrived Eddie stepped in. He

knew the bus driver. He often rode with him. His name was Mike.

"Hi!" said Mike. "You look like a movie actor. All you need is a carnation in your buttonhole. Where you going, all dressed up?"

"Don't ask me," Eddie moaned. He flopped into the seat nearest the door.

"Come on, tell me. You'll feel better if you tell me," said Mike.

"You promise you won't tell anybody?" said Eddie.

"On my honor," said Mike.

Eddie got up and whispered in Mike's ear. "I'm going to dancing school. Isn't that horrible?"

"Oh! Cheer up!" said Mike. "I went to dancing school once. And look at me now."

"You did?" said Eddie, with a brighter face. He leaned over and whispered, "And did you have pumps?"

"Sure! Sure!" said Mike. "I was the best pumper in the crowd. You'll learn to pump. It's easy."

"No, Mike," said Eddie. "They're some kind of shoes. They're in this package."

"Oh, I thought that was your supper," said Mike. "Oh, sure! Pumps. Sure, you gotta have pumps."

"I have to change buses at Brewster Road," said Eddie.

"Righto!" said Mike. "Three more stops before we get there."

When the bus reached Brewster Road, Mike drew up to the curb. As Eddie stepped out he said, "So long, Mike."

"So long, pal!" said Mike. "I'll wait for you to cross the street."

Eddie crossed the street in front of the bus. When he reached the opposite corner, he heard Mike calling, "Hey, Eddie!"

Eddie looked back and saw a package flying toward him. It landed at his feet. "Your pumps," Mike called out, as he started the bus.

Eddie picked up the parcel and put it under his arm. He stood on the corner and waited for the other bus. Across the street there was a used car lot. It belonged to Mr. Ward, a friend of Eddie's father. Eddie looked over the cars while he waited. Suddenly, he caught sight of something bright red. Eddie's heart began to beat faster. He ran across the street and over to the lot. Sure enough! It was just what he thought. There was the fire engine he had ridden on at the Fair. A man was lying under it, working with a hammer.

Eddie stooped down and looked under. There was Mr. Ward. "Hello, Mr. Ward!" said Eddie. "I rode on this fire engine once. It was super!"

"You did, Eddie?" said Mr. Ward, pushing himself out from between the wheels. "Well, how would you like to ride on it again?"

"Now?" said Eddie, his eyes shining.

"I want to see how it runs," said Mr. Ward. "I just put in a new part."

"Swell!" said Eddie, climbing right up into the front seat. "This is great!" he added, as the fire engine started.

Then Mr. Ward looked down on the ground. "Does that bundle belong to you?" he asked.

"Oh, golly! Yes," said Eddie. "Stop."

The fire engine stopped and Eddie got down. He ran back and picked up his package. Then he climbed up again. He put the package on the seat beside him and they started off. "I sure like this fire engine," he said.

"You going anywhere special?" Mr. Ward asked.

"Oh, not very special," Eddie replied.

"Got plenty of time?" said Mr. Ward.

"Oh sure!" said Eddie.

"Very well! She's going good. We'll take a spin around," said Mr. Ward.

Eddie held onto the seat and swung his legs. This was wonderful! "Can I pull the bell?" he asked.

"No, we can't ring the bell," said Mr. Ward. "The fire company would object. Might look like a false alarm."

Mr. Ward drove Eddie way out into the country before he said, "I guess I had better get back. Where can I drop you?"

Eddie thought of dancing school for the first time since he had been on the bus. "Oh! I have to go to Beech Tree Road," he said.

"Beech Tree Road?" said Mr. Ward. "What's going on there? By the way, you look all slicked up."

"Yeah," said Eddie. "I forgot all about it. I'm going to dancing school."

"You don't say!" said Mr. Ward. "What have you got in the package?"

Eddie looked sheepish. "Aw, pumps," he said.

"Pumps!" said Mr. Ward. "What the heck are pumps?"

"I don't know," said Eddie. "Something you wear on your feet."

"Well, suppose I take you right over to the place," said Mr. Ward.

"Oh, that would be great!" said Eddie.

Mrs. Wallace was standing at the front door when Eddie drove up in the fire engine. As he jumped down she said, "Why, Eddie! You're very late. I've been wondering why you didn't get here."

"I guess I am a little late," said Eddie. "Mr. Ward gave me a lift."

Eddie could hear the boys and girls laughing. They were all in the dining room.

"It's too bad you missed the dancing class," said Mrs. Wallace. "The children are having their ice cream now."

Eddie's face shone. "Ice cream?" he said. "Gee, that's great!"

"Hello, Eddie!" the children called out when Eddie walked into the dining room.

"Hello!" said Eddie, sitting down at the table.

Mrs. Wallace handed him a large plate of ice cream and Eddie lost no time in eating it. Just as he swallowed the last spoonful, the doorbell rang. Mrs. Wallace went to the front door and opened it. Eddie heard Mr. Ward's voice say, "Is Eddie Wilson still here?"

"Yes, he is," said Mrs. Wallace.

"Well, here are his pumps," said Mr. Ward.

The children had caught a glimpse of the fire engine through the open door. They rushed to the door to look at it. "Oh, here's the fire engine that was at the Fair!" they cried.

"I had a ride on it this afternoon," said Eddie.

"Oh, can we have a ride?" the children shouted. "Can we have a ride?"

"You have on your best clothes," said Mrs. Wallace. "You can't go riding on a fire engine in your best clothes, in your dancing clothes."

"We won't hurt them," the children cried.

"I didn't hurt mine, did I?" said Eddie.

"I'll take them all home," said Mr. Ward.

The children rushed to the fire engine, the little girls in their ruffled dresses and the boys in their Sunday suits.

"Now, everybody sit still," said Mr. Ward. "You have to keep your clothes clean."

Just as everyone was settled Eddie jumped down. "Wait a minute," he said.

He ran into the house and came back with his package. He looked up at Mr. Ward and grinned. "Forgot my pumps," he said.

Mr. Ward dropped the children off, one by one. Eddie was the last. When he drove up to the house, the twins were looking out of the window. When they saw Eddie, they rushed to the front door.

"What's the idea," cried Joe, "riding on the fire engine?"

"Where have you been?" cried Frank.

"I've been to dancing school," said Eddie.

"Dancing school!" cried the twins in chorus.

"Gee, it's swell!" said Eddie, as he waved good-by to Mr. Ward.

When dinner was almost over, the doorbell rang. Mr. Wilson went to the door and opened it and everyone around the dining-room table heard Mr. Ward's voice say, "Here are Eddie's pumps. He left them on the fire engine."

When Mr. Wilson came back to the dining room, he was carrying a package. He put it on the window sill. "Here are your pumps, Eddie," he said.

"Pumps!" cried Rudy and the twins together. "What are pumps?"

"I don't know," said Eddie. "I haven't had time to look at 'em. But dancing school was swell, Mama. Dancing school was swell!"

Chapter Five

Anna Patricia's Teeth

It was true that Anna Patricia had been without her upper front teeth for a very long time. She had come to Eddie's school from another city. No one thought anything about Anna Patricia's missing teeth at first, because nearly everyone in the second grade had one or two teeth out. In fact, when Anna Patricia joined the class Eddie didn't have any upper or lower front teeth. But new ones soon began to appear and by the end of the term the spaces were filled up.

When the boys and girls returned to school

in September, Anna Patricia was the only one with teeth still missing.

When Eddie saw her, he said, "Geepers! Aren't you ever going to get any teeth?"

"Don't be tho rude, Eddie Wilthon," said Anna Patricia. "Of courth I'm going to get teeth. And they'll be beautiful, too."

But days and weeks went by and there was no sign of Anna Patricia's new teeth. Soon Eddie and all the other boys in the class were calling Anna Patricia "Toothless." But Anna Patricia did not mind very much. Nearly everyone had a nickname and some were worse than Toothless.

They called George Mason Fish-face and they had called him that so long that no one remembered how it started. Then there were Boodles Cary and Chicken-feet Foster and Dumpty Peterson. So Anna Patricia did not mind being called Toothless very much, because some day she would have beautiful teeth, as beautiful as the children's in the movies. Then they wouldn't call her Toothless any more. They would call her Anna Patricia, just as her mother and father did.

One morning Anna Patricia rushed into her classroom and shouted, "Look!"

Everyone turned to look at Anna Patricia. She grinned a very wide grin. "I've got teeth," she said.

No one made any fuss over Anna Patricia's

having teeth so suddenly. They all had teeth of their own and it was high time Anna Patricia had some too. But when Anna Patricia shouted, "I can take 'em out," every child in the room rushed up to her.

"Let's see you," cried Eddie.

"I'm not allowed," said Anna Patricia.

"Aw, I don't believe they come out," said Eddie.

"They do so," said Anna Patricia.

"Well, take 'em out then. Take 'em out," said Boodles, "and let's see."

"I'm not allowed to take them out," said Anna Patricia. "I'm not allowed to take them out unless they hurt me."

"Can't you make 'em hurt?" said Eddie.

"Where did you get them?" asked Janie Jamison.

"My daddy made them for me. My daddy is a dentist," said Anna Patricia. "I broke my front teeth just before we moved here and he said he guessed I wasn't going to get any more. So he made these for me. He says lots of movie actresses have them. So now I'm just like a movie actress."

"How do they stay in?" Eddie asked.

"They hook on to my other teeth," she said.

"Let's see," said Eddie.

Anna Patricia threw back her head and opened her mouth very wide. Eddie stooped down and looked inside. "Say! They do!" he cried. "What do you know about that!"

"Let me see," said a boy named John Baker, pushing Eddie aside. "Let me see the hooks."

At that moment the bell rang for school to begin. "Boys and girls," said Miss Weber, their teacher, "leave Anna Patricia's teeth alone and take your seats."

At recess the children gathered around Anna Patricia. They all wanted to see her new teeth.

"I'll give you a caramel," said Eddie, "if you'll take 'em out, just once."

Anna Patricia shook her head.

"I'll give you two caramels," said Eddie.

Anna Patricia loved caramels. In fact, caramels were her favorite kind of candy. She thought for a few minutes. Then she said, "Well, they do hurt me a little."

The crowd moved closer to Anna Patricia. She was in the midst of speechless boys and girls. With wide eyes they watched Anna Patricia take hold of her two little teeth. With one pull, out they came.

The whole crowd sighed. "Gee!" said Eddie. "I wish I could do that."

Anna Patricia popped them back in again and said, "Now where are my caramels, Eddie?"

Eddie handed over the two caramels and Anna Patricia removed the paper covering from one of them. She put the whole caramel into her mouth and began to chew. Suddenly she clapped her hand over her mouth and her eyes looked frightened.

"What's the matter?" Eddie asked.

Anna Patricia kept her hand over her mouth. "Uh carm ith thuck um muh feef," she said.

"Let's see," said Eddie.

Anna Patricia shook her head so hard her curls hit Eddie in the face.

"Go in to Miss Weber," said Janie. "Go on in to Miss Weber."

Anna Patricia, with her hand over her mouth, started in to find Miss Weber. The crowd followed her. In a few minutes they reached their classroom. Miss Weber was writing on the blackboard. "Whatever is the matter?" she asked.

"Anna Patricia's teeth are stuck on her caramel," said Janie.

"Well, everybody go back to the yard," said Miss Weber. "I'll take care of Anna Patricia."

The children were sorry to leave but they had to do what Miss Weber told them. Then Miss Weber took Anna Patricia into her dressing room and in a few minutes Anna Patricia's little teeth were back where they belonged.

Anna Patricia decided to spend the rest of her recess time in the room. She sat down at her desk and began to read a book. She put her other caramel on top of her desk. She wanted very much to eat it, but she didn't want the same trouble that she had had with the first caramel. She decided not to run any risk, so she took her little pearly front teeth out and wrapped them in a piece of tissue paper. Then she put the tiny package on her desk, right beside her inkwell.

Anna Patricia was just finishing her second caramel when the children returned from recess. As soon as they were settled in their places, Miss Weber started the arithmetic lesson. She called Anna Patricia to the blackboard to write the answer to 36 divided by 6. As Anna Patricia rose, her arm swept across her desk. She walked up to the blackboard and wrote a large 6 for the answer.

Miss Weber said, "That is right, Anna Patricia. You may go to the modeling table and work on your modeling."

Anna Patricia was delighted to get to the modeling table. She loved to model. She was modeling a squirrel with a bushy tail. She was so happy at her work that she thought of nothing else and it seemed a very short time when the luncheon bell sounded.

Anna Patricia washed her hands and followed the rest of the children to the lunchroom. It was a cafeteria and Anna Patricia stood behind Eddie with her tray. She bought a sandwich, a bowl of soup, and a cup of cocoa. She bought some chocolate pudding and two cookies for dessert. Anna Patricia carried her tray to a table near the water cooler and sat down beside Janie.

Miss Weber ate her lunch quickly and returned to her classroom to mark the spelling papers. She had just finished the last paper when she heard someone crying.

She got up and went into the hall. A crowd of children, with Anna Patricia in the center, came rushing down the hall. Anna Patricia was wailing at the top of her lungs. Before Miss Weber could ask what the trouble was, Eddie called out, "Anna Patricia swallowed her new teeth."

"Oh, Anna Patricia!" said Miss Weber. "You couldn't have swallowed your teeth."

"But I did, I did," wailed Anna Patricia.

Miss Weber took Anna Patricia into her room. She sent the rest of the children back to the lunchroom.

"Now, Anna Patricia," said Miss Weber, "when did you last have your teeth?"

"I don't remember," sobbed Anna Patricia. "I wath eating my thandwich and all of a thudden I didn't feel them."

"Well, you couldn't have swallowed them," said Miss Weber.

"But I haven't got them," Anna Patricia wailed.

"You must have put them somewhere," said Miss Weber. "If you had swallowed them, you would have felt them go down."

"Then where are they?" cried Anna Patricia.

"I wish I knew," said Miss Weber. "We shall have to look for them."

Just then the bell rang and the children came trooping in from lunch. Anna Patricia had stopped her sobbing and was rubbing the tears from her eyes. When the children were seated, Miss Weber said, "Boys and girls, does anyone remember seeing Anna Patricia's teeth?"

There wasn't a sound out of anyone.

"Well, we must find them," said Miss Weber. "I want every boy and girl in this room to take everything out of his or her desk. Eddie, I want you to get a long-handled brush from the janitor and sweep up the floor. And I want George to empty the wastepaper basket and open up any pieces of crumpled paper. Anna Patricia, clear up everything on the modeling table and see if they are there."

Eddie took everything out of his desk and then went off to get the long-handled floor brush. George set to work emptying the scrap basket. Every once in a while Anna Patricia could be heard to sob.

"I hope, Anna Patricia," said Miss Weber, "that after we find them you will keep them where they belong."

"Yeth, Mith Weber," said Anna Patricia.

The contents of every desk were looked over. George went through every scrap of paper in the wastebasket and Eddie swept the floor very carefully, but Anna Patricia's little teeth did not turn up. Anna Patricia cleaned up the whole of the modeling table, and when she failed to find them she began to cry again.

"Stop crying, Anna Patricia," said Miss Weber. "Your teeth can't be out of this room. We'll find them and we'll stay here until we do. I want every boy to empty his pockets and put everything he finds on his desk."

The boys dug into their pockets, and piles of odds and ends began to appear on their desks. There were enough nails, it seemed, to build a house and enough nuts and bolts to put an automobile together. There were enough washers and stoppers to keep a plumber happy for a year. Marbles and bottle tops fell to the floor and rolled into corners. There were enough radio parts to set up a repair shop and Miss Weber said that the string that came out of the boys' pockets was enough to tie up an elephant. But Anna Patricia's teeth were not found among these treasures.

Suddenly Eddie had an idea. "Let's look in the inkwells," he said.

"Very well," said Miss Weber. "We have looked everywhere else. Everyone dip the end of his paintbrush into his inkwell. Do it carefully. And let it drip on your blotter when you take it out, not on the desk or on the floor."

The children dipped their paintbrushes into the inkwells. They stirred the ink very carefully.

Anna Patricia stirred the end of her paintbrush around in her inkwell. It was hard to stir. The ink seemed to be soaked up and something soft and mushy was in the bottom of the inkwell. Then her brush bumped into something hard. In a moment it caught on a hook and, very carefully, Anna Patricia lifted her little teeth out of her inkwell. "Here they are!" she cried, holding them up, as drops of ink fell on her blotter. "Here they are!"

"Well, I *am* glad," said Miss Weber. "Now

go and scrub them with soap and water, and when they're clean put them where they belong and keep them there."

As Anna Patricia left the room, carrying her teeth on a blotter, Eddie cried, "Gee! They certainly look as though they had been eating blueberries."

As the door closed behind Anna Patricia, Boodles Cary called out, "Nuisance, aren't they?"

And Miss Weber replied, "They certainly are. I'm glad the rest of you have your teeth fastened in."

Chapter Six

Eddie's Christmas Card

It was about two weeks before Christmas. The shop windows were filled with Christmas gifts, and inside and outside there were Christmas decorations. Along the main street Christmas greens and electric lights were looped from lamp post to lamp post. On the sidings down at the railroad station there were carloads of evergreen trees, waiting to be unloaded and taken to the stores.

The decorations at Mr. Ward's used car lot were the cause of great excitement. Eddie was the first to see them and he lost no time in spreading the news.

"You should see what Mr. Ward has done over at his car lot," said Eddie one morning when he reached school.

"What's he done?" the children cried.

"He has the fire engine right out in front, right on the corner. And guess what he has sitting at the wheel of the fire engine!"

"What?" the children asked.

"Santa Claus!" shouted Eddie.

That afternoon, as soon as school was over, the children rushed over to Mr. Ward's car lot. Sure enough, there under a big wide banner stretched between two poles stood the fire engine, and at the wheel sat a funny little stuffed body, dressed like Santa Claus. On the banner were the words *Merry Christmas*.

"He's a gnome Santa Claus," said Anna Patricia. "He isn't any bigger than Eddie."

The children climbed up on the fire engine to get better acquainted with Santa Claus. They laughed and shouted.

"He's made of a potato sack stuffed with

rags," cried Boodles.

"His beard is made of cotton," shouted George.

"Shake hands, Santa Claus," Eddie said, as he pumped Santa Claus's limp right arm up and down.

"Handle Santa Claus gently," Mr. Ward called out. "He's a little weak in spots." This made the children laugh.

"He's got an awfully funny hat on," said Anna Patricia. "The tassel sticks up in the air. It ought to hang down."

"Now see here," said Mr. Ward, "you mustn't criticize Santa Claus. You'll hurt his feelings."

"I think he's swell," said Eddie, sitting down on the seat beside Santa Claus.

That night, when Eddie got into his bed, he thought about Santa Claus and the fire engine and suddenly an idea came to him. He would get his father to take his photograph, sitting on the fire engine beside Santa Claus. And he would use the photographs for his Christmas cards. Eddie went to sleep with a smile on his face, thinking of how surprised the children in school would be when they received his Christmas card and saw him sitting beside Santa Claus on the fire engine.

He decided that he wouldn't tell anyone about his Christmas card, but it was hard to keep it a secret. Every once in a while he would say to one of his friends, "Just wait until you see my Christmas card. It's going to be super!"

Eddie could hardly wait to have his photograph taken, but his father was out of town so Eddie had to wait until the following Saturday.

Very early on Friday morning it began to snow. When Eddie and his brothers saw the snow, they were delighted. "Boy, oh, boy!" cried Frank. "Now we'll have some good sledding!"

"I sure hope it lasts over Christmas," cried Rudy, "so I can do some skiing with the skis I'm going to get."

When Rudy went to the back door to get the milk for his mother, he found the bottle of cream completely covered with snow. Only the milk bottles stuck up above the surface of the snow. "It sure is snowing," said Rudy, as he placed the milk and cream on the kitchen table. "It's snowing so hard you can hardly see as far as the corner."

By the time the boys started for school, the snow had covered the street and the sidewalks so that the curbstones had completely disappeared. The boys walked single file in the narrow path that had been made by people walking to the bus stop at the corner. At noon it was still snowing, harder than ever. So much snow had fallen that the children were dismissed from school. They were told to go straight home. The children departed, shouting with joy over the unexpected half holiday.

On Saturday morning when Eddie came downstairs he said, "Papa, are you going to take my picture with Santa Claus today?"

"Yes," replied Mr. Wilson, "this afternoon, right after lunch. We'll probably have to shovel the whole way and sweep the snow out of the fire engine."

"It sure is deep," said Eddie, "but it will be tramped down by this afternoon."

But by afternoon it had begun to snow again. "Can't take any pictures in this," said Mr. Wilson, when he came home. "We'll have to wait until tomorrow."

"Well, we'll have to take 'em tomorrow," said Eddie, "because I'm going to use the pictures for my Christmas cards."

On Sunday morning when Eddie looked out of the window, he thought it looked like the North Pole. Fences and hedges had completely disappeared and lawns, driveways, and street were all one even white blanket. Nothing stood above the surface of the snow but the houses, trees, and telephone poles. The first-floor windows in the house across the way seemed to Eddie to be peeping over the snow.

When Eddie went out of doors, he sank into the snow up to his waist and it was so heavy he could hardly move. "Papa!" said Eddie, when he came indoors. "Do you think we can take the picture?"

Mr. Wilson was trying to get the highway department at the Town Hall on the telephone. He wanted to find out whether the snowplow would be up their way soon. When he hung up the receiver he said, "They have no idea when they can get out here, maybe not until tonight."

"Oh, Papa," Eddie cried, "I have to have my picture taken with Santa Claus today. It's going to be my Christmas card."

"Eddie," said Mr. Wilson, "the fire engine is probably buried in the snow and Santa Claus with it."

"But what will I do about my Christmas card?" said Eddie.

"Couldn't you buy a few?" asked his father.

"They wouldn't be me and Santa Claus," said Eddie.

"That's so," said Mr. Wilson. "But is it important that it should be you and Santa Claus?"

"Oh, it's very important," said Eddie. "Nobody else has thought of it but me. My

Christmas card will be different from everybody else's."

"And is it important for your Christmas card to be different from all the others?" said his father.

"Uh-huh," said Eddie, with the grin that always made his father laugh.

"Well, if we can ever get out of here, we'll go over this afternoon and see how things are," said Mr. Wilson. "Meanwhile we'd better get the driveway shoveled out before the plow comes through and throws another ton of snow on top of us. Come on, boys!"

Each of the boys got a shovel and Mr. Wilson and his four helpers set to work to clear the driveway. The snow was so deep they had to take it off in layers. They worked for twenty minutes and then rested ten minutes all through the morning. They stopped for dinner and Mother said they all ate like bears. In the afternoon they finished their work and by half past two the driveway was shoveled all the way down to the curb.

"What do we do now?" said Eddie, surveying the thick white mass that filled the street.

Before anyone could answer, the snowplow came around the corner, cutting its way through the snow and piling it into a wall on the sidewalk. Eddie watched the plow as it came nearer and nearer. The men on the plow were waving their arms and shouting. Eddie waved his arms and shouted, too.

"Get back," cried Eddie's father. "Eddie, get back." But Eddie was too much interested in watching the plow to hear.

Mr. Wilson rushed up to Eddie and grabbed him by the arm, just as the plow reached their driveway. With a great swish, the snow flew into the open drive and in a second Eddie and his father had so much snow sticking to them that they looked like a couple of snow men.

By the time the snow that the plow had thrown into the drive had been cleared away, it was three o'clock. Rudy and the twins went into the house, took off their things, and fell sound asleep. But not little Eddie. He was all ready to have his picture taken. So Mr. Wilson got the car out of the garage and he and Eddie drove over to Mr. Ward's used car lot. They almost passed it, for all the cars were completely covered with snow. There were only slight bumps to show their tops. The fire engine had disappeared altogether. A little red tassel that seemed to be resting on the surface of the snow was the only thing that showed where the fire engine was.

"What do you suppose that red thing is?" Mr. Wilson asked.

"Why, that's the tassel on Santa Claus's hat!" cried Eddie.

"You can't have your picture taken with Santa Claus today," said Mr. Wilson.

"Well, take the picture anyway," said Eddie.

So Mr. Wilson took the picture.

About three days before Christmas, Eddie began to receive Christmas cards. In the first envelope was a photograph of Anna Patricia sitting beside Santa Claus on the fire engine.

On the back of the card it said, "Merry Christmas from Anna Patricia and Santa Claus."

When Eddie looked at George's card, there was George sitting up on the fire engine beside Santa Claus. It said, "Merry Christmas from Santa Claus and George."

When Betsy's card arrived, Eddie read, "Betsy and Star with Santa Claus. Merry Christmas." Santa Claus was sitting between Betsy and Star.

The day before Christmas, Eddie received a card from Boodles. It said, "Me and Santa Claus driving the fire engine. Merry Christmas! Boodles."

In the afternoon a card came from Lilly. There was Lilly, sitting beside Santa Claus on the fire engine. It said, "Lilly and Santa Claus wish you a Merry Christmas."

On Christmas Day all of Eddie's friends received his Christmas card. On the back of each one Eddie had printed his message.

SANTA CLAUS On The FIRE
ENGINE WITHOUT ME.
MERRYCHRISTMAS FROM
EDDIE

And everyone who received a card from
Eddie saw that Eddie was not there and they
wondered where Santa Claus and the fire
engine were. And what was that tiny speck
sticking up out of the snow?

"That," said Eddie, when they asked him
about it, "is the tassel on Santa Claus's hat. He's
under it."

When Mr. Kilpatrick saw Eddie he said,
"Thank you for your Christmas card, Eddie. I
liked it very much."

Eddie said, "I liked it, too. It was different."

"That's what I said to Mrs. Kilpatrick, the
very words. I said, 'Now here's Eddie Wilson's
card. That's a fine card. Trust little Eddie to be
different.'"

Chapter Seven

How Santa Claus Delivered Presents

Every year an enormous Christmas tree was placed on the grounds in front of the Town Hall. It was strung with hundreds of blue electric lights and on the very tiptop there was a brilliant white star. The lights were always turned on at five o'clock on Christmas Eve and nearly everyone who lived in the town, and even people who lived out in the country, gathered in the square and sang Christmas carols.

Right on the edge of the town there was a large orphanage and the children always came to the Christmas party. After the carol singing each child received a present.

Eddie's father was in charge of the Town Hall Christmas party this year and the Wilson boys were thrilled. They all felt like Santa Claus's helpers and Eddie felt like Santa Claus himself. One of the most exciting things was getting the big Christmas tree. Mr. Wilson told the boys that they could go with him to get it and Eddie could hardly wait for the day to arrive.

"Where do we have to go for it?" Eddie asked one evening.

"Over to the railroad freight station about two miles from here," said Mr. Wilson. "It will be tagged for Town Hall. It's always cut especially for the purpose. In fact, it's always one of the largest trees in the country."

"You mean in the whole United States?" said Eddie.

"That's right," his father replied.

"Where do they cut such a big Christmas tree?" said Eddie.

"Up in Maine," replied Mr. Wilson. "They have to send it down on a railroad car that handles telegraph poles."

"How do they put up such a big tree in the square?" Eddie asked.

"Oh, the men who put up the telephone poles put it up," Mr. Wilson answered. "They offer to do it each year and the company lets them take the truck over to the station to get the tree."

"Oh, Papa!" Eddie cried. "I thought we were going for the tree."

"We are," said Mr. Wilson. "We are going over in our car, but the telephone men are going to do the hauling. Then we'll drive over to the square and watch them put it up. The workers from the electric company will string up the lights."

"Won't we do anything but watch 'em?" Eddie said, looking downcast.

"I think you will find plenty to do," said his father. "You usually do."

For weeks now, the boys and girls in school

had been busy repairing and painting toys they had brought. These were to be given out at the Christmas party to the children from the orphanage and in the hospital. The boys put new wheels on toy wagons and gave them fresh coats of paint so that they looked brand new. The girls made new dresses for the dolls that were brought to school and painted their faces and tied new ribbons on their hair. When they were all finished, the window sills in every class room were piled high with toys. No one would have been surprised to find Santa Claus himself walking up and down the halls of the school.

"How are we going to get all these toys over to the square?" Eddie asked one day.

"Mr. Ward has offered to take them over in the old fire engine," said Miss Weber.

"I wonder if he'll let Santa Claus drive them over," said Boodles, laughing.

"The fire engine and Santa Claus were buried in the snow the last time I passed Mr. Ward's," said Eddie. "All you could see was the tassel on Santa Claus's hat."

"Well, Mr. Ward has charge of the presents," said Miss Weber. "We don't have to worry about them. Mr. Ward said he would get them to the Christmas party and distribute them. I am sure he'll find a way to do it even if his fire engine is buried in the snow."

That afternoon after school Eddie walked over to Mr. Ward's used car lot. He found Mr. Ward digging the fire engine out of the snow. "Have you got another shovel, Mr. Ward?" Eddie asked. "If you have, I'll help you."

"I certainly have, Eddie," said Mr. Ward, "and I'd be mighty glad of a little help."

"O.K.," said Eddie and when Mr. Ward got the shovel, he set to work.

"I hear you're going to take the toys over to the square on Christmas Eve," said Eddie.

"That's right," Mr. Ward replied. "That's why I have to dig this out of the snow."

"Are you going to take Santa Claus?" asked Eddie.

"Oh, sure!" replied Mr. Ward. "Santa Claus has to go to the big Christmas doings. Santa

Claus has to give out the presents."

"But he can't," said Eddie, "'cause he's only stuffed."

"Well, I've got an idea," said Mr. Ward.

"What is it?" Eddie asked.

Mr. Ward leaned on his shovel while he told Eddie his idea and Eddie stopped shoveling to listen. Eddie's eyes grew larger and his smile grew broader as Mr. Ward's idea unfolded.

Finally Mr. Ward said, "What do you think of that, Eddie?"

Eddie replied, "I think it's super! Positively super! I can hardly wait!"

"Well now, don't tell anyone," said Mr. Ward.

"Not even my father?" said Eddie.

"Oh, I've already talked to your father about it. He thinks it's a swell idea."

"Geepers! I can hardly wait," said Eddie, as he dug his shovel into the snow.

Finally the day arrived for the big Christmas tree to be put up in the square. Mr. Wilson left his office early and reached home about the same time as Eddie and his brothers. They had come straight home from school for they didn't want their father to go for the tree without them. The four boys climbed into the car and Mr. Wilson started for the railroad station where the Christmas tree was waiting.

"Do you think we'll get there before the telephone men, Papa?" said Eddie. "You don't think they'll get there first and take it away before we get there, do you?"

"They may get there first," said Mr. Wilson, "but they can't take the tree until I get there because I have to sign the receipt for it. It was shipped in my name."

"That's good," said Eddie. "I want to see them put the Christmas tree on the truck."

Just then Mr. Wilson drove around a bend in the road and there, ahead of them, was the telephone truck. It was parked at the side of the road and the telephone men had their heads inside the hood.

Mr. Wilson drove up behind them and stopped his car. He got out and walked to the truck. Eddie and his brothers got out and followed him.

"Hello, boys!" said Mr. Wilson. "What's the trouble?"

"Oh, hello, Mr. Wilson," said one of the men. "Got some trouble with the truck. Seems to be in the motor."

"She's as dead as a herring," said another man. "They'll have to tow her in."

"How will we get the Christmas tree?" asked Rudy.

"We can call up Mr. Ward," said Eddie. "He'll bring the fire engine over."

"Now, Eddie, this is one time we are not going to get the fire engine out," said his father. "Mr. Ward's fire engine isn't long enough to take the tree."

"Tell you what, Mr. Wilson," said the man that the other two called Pete, "suppose you drive me back to town. I'll pick up the tow truck and I'll come back for this truck and maybe I can think of a way to get the tree hauled over."

"Very well," said Mr. Wilson, "we'll start right back."

Meanwhile, Eddie kept saying, "Papa, I think Mr. Ward's fire engine is big enough. Why don't you call him?"

Finally Mr. Wilson said, "Now, Eddie, forget it. I know it wouldn't be big enough, so forget it. You're not going to ride on the fire engine tonight."

As Mr. Wilson and Pete walked toward the Wilsons' car, the other two men said, "We'll wait here."

"O.K.!" said Pete. "We won't be more than a half hour. You'd better put some flares in the road so you won't get hit."

"We'll build a bonfire too, so we won't freeze before you get back," said one of the men.

When Rudy and the twins heard there was to be a bonfire they decided to stay with the truck, but Eddie climbed back into his father's car.

"Can I ride back on the tow truck?" he said to Pete as soon as Mr. Wilson had turned the car around.

"Sure!" said Pete.

Mr. Wilson hadn't quite reached the edge of the town when Pete said, "You know what? I'll bet the boys at the firehouse would go over for that tree with the hook and ladder truck."

"That's an idea!" said Mr. Wilson. "Maybe they would. Let's stop and ask them."

"Oh, boy!" cried Eddie. "This is going to be super!"

Mr. Wilson drove up to the firehouse where the hook and ladder was kept and he and Pete and Eddie went in. Mr. Wilson and Pete knew all the firemen and when Mr. Wilson told them what he wanted, they said, "It's O.K. with us, but you'll have to ask the Chief. He's gone home to dinner."

In a few minutes Mr. Wilson had the Chief on the telephone.

"It's O.K. with me," said the Chief. "But you'll have to ask the mayor." So Mr. Wilson telephoned to the mayor, and when the mayor heard the story he said, "Sure! Tell the boys to take the hook and ladder over. We have to get the tree." Mr. Wilson telephoned the Chief again.

It was no time at all before the firemen, in their heavy coats, were ready to drive the big shiny red hook and ladder out of the firehouse. Eddie was so excited he was hopping up and down on one foot.

"Do you want to come along?" one of the firemen called to him.

"Oh yes!" cried Eddie.

"Are you bundled up good and warm?" the fireman asked.

"Sure!" said Eddie, as one of the men lifted him up beside the driver.

"Better put these ear muffs on," said one of the men, and he put an enormous pair of ear muffs on Eddie's head.

Eddie looked as though his face was being held between the paws of a great big bear, with a grin stretching from one paw to the other.

"This is super!" cried Eddie, as he waved good-by to his father and Pete.

"I'll meet you over at the station," Mr. Wilson called. "I'll drop Pete off for his truck."

Rudy and the twins and the two telephone men were warming themselves by the fire when they heard the rumbling of a heavy truck approaching. "Guess this is them," said Rudy.

"Sounds too heavy," said one of the men, looking at the oncoming headlights.

"I'll be hanged if it isn't the boys from the firehouse with the hook and ladder!" said the other man, as the firemen drew up behind the telephone company truck.

"Hi!" cried Eddie to his brothers.

"Look at Eddie!" cried Frank.

"Hey! How do you get that way?" cried Rudy.

"Are you going after the Christmas tree?" Joe asked.

"You bet we are!" the driver called. "When you want to get something done in these parts, you have to get the fire company to do it." Everyone laughed.

"Can we come too?" Frank asked.

"Sure! Everybody up," the driver of the hook and ladder called out.

Eddie's brothers scrambled up, and the hook and ladder started off again. The telephone men shouted "So long!" and waved.

The firemen and the boys waved back. "We'll send a horse and sleigh to tow you in," one of the firemen shouted and everyone laughed.

It was not long before the firemen pulled up alongside of the freight station. They all jumped down.

"Where's this Christmas tree we have to haul over to the Town Hall?" the driver asked the man in charge of the freight station.

"Right over on the siding," said the man. "I'll show you."

By the time the firemen had the tree fastened on the hook and ladder, Mr. Wilson had arrived. He signed the receipt for the tree, while the boys climbed back up with the firemen.

"Anybody driving back to town with me?" Mr. Wilson asked.

No one made any reply. "Guess not!" said Mr. Wilson.

"You'll have to get yourself a fire engine, Mr. Wilson, if you want somebody to ride with you," said the freight station man.

"Looks that way," said Mr. Wilson.

When the firemen and the Wilson boys arrived in front of the Town Hall with the Christmas tree, the telephone men were waiting to put it up. In a very short time they had the big tree in place. As the hook and ladder drove away, the men from the electric company arrived with yards and yards and yards of electric cord and hundreds of blue bulbs.

It was nine o'clock before the job was finished, and then Mr. Wilson suddenly remembered that he and the boys had forgotten all about dinner. He ran to the nearest telephone and called up Mrs. Wilson. When he heard her voice he said, "I'm terribly sorry, but I forgot all about dinner. We've been so busy with the Christmas tree."

"I thought you would," said Mrs. Wilson, "so I baked beans. They're in the oven and it doesn't make any difference if they stay there until next week."

"Baked beans!" cried Mr. Wilson. "I hope you baked a bushel. Have you got enough for twelve hungry men, including Eddie?"

"I believe so," said Mrs. Wilson, laughing. "Bring them over."

Mr. Wilson went outside and called, "Hey, there are baked beans at our house. Come along, everybody!"

The following evening, about five o'clock, the square in front of the Town Hall was thronged with people. Every face was turned toward the huge Christmas tree. From the belfry of a near-by church came the sound of chimes playing "O little town of Bethlehem." As the hands of the Town Hall clock pointed to five o'clock, the lights on the Christmas tree were turned on. The blue lights seemed suddenly to turn the square into fairyland.

For fifteen minutes the chimes played and all the people in the square sang Christmas carols. When the singing was over, Mr. Wilson spoke from the steps of the Town Hall. He said, "Santa Claus is now driving into the square with his fire engine full of presents for some of our very good boys and girls."

Betsy, who was standing with her mother and Star, looked where Mr. Wilson was pointing and she saw Mr. Ward driving his fire engine very slowly up to the entrance of the Town Hall. On the seat beside Mr. Ward, leaning against him, was the funny little Santa Claus Mr. Ward had made. When Mr. Ward stood up, Santa Claus toppled right over in a heap and everyone laughed. Then Mr. Ward picked up Santa Claus and handed him down to Mr. Wilson who tucked him under his arm and carried him up the steps of the Town Hall. There he deposited him on the wide brick wall and propped him up against a post. Santa Claus doubled up like a jackknife.

"Now see here, Santa Claus," said Mr. Wilson, "this is Christmas Eve and you have work to do. You'll have to come to life. Just look at all these boys and girls waiting for you

to give them their presents." And Mr. Wilson shook Santa Claus very hard.

The children gathered in front of the steps shouted with laughter, but their laughter was soon stopped by their surprise. Very slowly Santa Claus began to straighten up. He stretched one arm out and then the other. Then he began to get up, and suddenly there was a lively little Santa Claus standing on his feet and calling out, "Merry Christmas! Merry Christmas! Step right up, boys and girls, and get your presents!"

"Why," shouted Betsy, "it's little Eddie! It's little Eddie!"

Chapter Eight

Eddie and the Goat

Eddie had not brought home a stray dog or cat for a long time. In fact, it had been such a long time that his father and mother had almost forgotten that Eddie had often had three and four cats at one time. But they had not quite forgotten.

For the past week the children in Eddie's class had been having the fun of owning a baby goat. A farmer who was a friend of Miss Weber's had given the baby goat to her and she had brought it to school. The children had been reading the story of Heidi and they were all interested in Heidi's goat. Of course the children wanted the little goat to stay at school forever, but Miss Weber said she would have to take it back to the farmer, because there really was no place to keep a goat.

"Couldn't we keep it where we have it now?" George asked. "Out back of the school on the grass?"

"Couldn't we build a house for it?" asked Eddie.

"No," said Miss Weber, "we can't keep the goat here. But the farmer said that if anyone would like to have the goat and would take proper care of it, he'd be glad to give it away."

Eddie could hardly believe his ears. "You mean for nothing?" he cried.

"That's what the farmer told me," said Miss Weber.

"Well, I could have it," said Eddie. "I could keep it at my house. I could take care of it."

"Are you sure, Eddie?" Miss Weber asked. "Are you sure your father and mother wouldn't object to your having the goat?"

"Oh, sure!" said Eddie. "Sure! My father and mother love goats. They'd be delighted to have a little goat."

"I think you had better ask them first," said Miss Weber.

"I don't have to ask them," said Eddie. "I can take the goat."

"Ask them first," said Miss Weber.

At dinner that night Eddie said, "Papa, you know the baby goat I told you about?"

Mr. Wilson said, "What about the baby goat, Eddie?"

"Well, it's an awful nice little goat," said Eddie. "I could have a very enjoyable time with that little goat."

"A goat!" exclaimed Mr. Wilson. "That's just what we need! A goat! Probably the only way we can ever get rid of the junk in the basement—get a goat to eat it!" And at this point Mr. Wilson got up to go to a meeting. "Yes indeed!" he said. "A goat is just what we need!"

The following day when Eddie went to

school he said, "Miss Weber, I can have the goat. My father said it was just what we need."

"Very well, Eddie, the goat is yours," said Miss Weber. "Take it away this afternoon."

"I brought a dog collar and a leash," said Eddie. "Do you think she'll go with me?"

Miss Weber thought the goat would go with Eddie and it did. And a whole crowd of children went too. But Eddie had a hard time walking with the goat, because the goat was always walking sideways instead of forward. This made the going very slow and the children were always bumping into each other because the goat bumped into them. One by one they left Eddie until he and the goat were alone.

The closer Eddie got to his home the more he thought of his father, and the more he thought of his father the more he felt that he was not going to like the little goat. There was something about the way Father had said, "A goat is just what we need," that made Eddie feel perhaps he would not be pleased.

Eddie decided to sit down on the curbstone

and think the matter over. The goat lay down beside him. Here Mr. Kilpatrick found them as he was driving home in his red police car.

Mr. Kilpatrick stopped and said, "What are you doing with the goat, Eddie?"

"I was taking her home but now I don't know. I'm afraid maybe my father won't like it." Then Eddie told Mr. Kilpatrick how he had happened to get the goat.

"Did you ask your father whether you could bring the goat home?" Mr. Kilpatrick asked.

"Well, not exactly," said Eddie. "I told him we had a goat at school and he said, 'That's just what we need, a goat!'"

"He did?" said Mr. Kilpatrick, raising his eyebrows. "That doesn't sound so good to me."

"You don't think he'll like the goat, Mr. Kilpatrick?" said Eddie, looking up at the big policeman.

Mr. Kilpatrick shook his head. "I have me doubts," he said, "very grave doubts."

Eddie sat with his chin resting in the palm of his hand. The little goat nuzzled its nose under

Eddie's arm. Eddie patted it on the head. "I think if my father knew this little goat, he would like her," he said.

"Sure, maybe!" said Mr. Kilpatrick. "But you made a big mistake in not talking to him about it first. You should have told him all the nice things about the goat and got him interested. You should have smoothed the way. That's what you call diplomacy. If you take this goat home now, your father will probably throw it out."

"Out where?" said Eddie, with a startled face.

Mr. Kilpatrick waved his arms around. "Oh, he'll probably telephone for the S.P.C.A."

"What's that?" Eddie asked.

"The Society for the Prevention of Cruelty to Animals," said Mr. Kilpatrick.

"But I'm not going to be cruel to my goat," said Eddie.

"Nevertheless," said Mr. Kilpatrick, "that's where it will go. I can see it in my mind's eye. You should have used diplomacy."

Eddie sat deep in thought. The goat was

taking a nap. Mr. Kilpatrick sat in his red car, looking down at the two on the curb.

In a few minutes Eddie looked up. His face was brighter. "Mr. Kilpatrick," he said, "couldn't you keep my goat until I can use what you said on my father? I don't want my goat to go to the Cruelty to Animals."

This surprised Mr. Kilpatrick very much indeed. "Oh, Mrs. Kilpatrick wouldn't like it," he said. "She wouldn't like it at all."

"But it would only be until tomorrow. I could talk to Papa tonight," said Eddie.

Mr. Kilpatrick thought for a few minutes. Then he said, "Well, come on. We'll take it along. We'll see whether Mrs. Kilpatrick will have it overnight."

Eddie got up and this woke the goat. He lifted it in his arms and put it on the front seat, between Mr. Kilpatrick and himself. In a moment they were off. They turned a few corners and the car stopped in front of Mr. Kilpatrick's white picket fence.

Mrs. Kilpatrick was cutting flowers in her

garden. She looked up when the car stopped and waved her hand. She watched Mr. Kilpatrick step out of the car and she watched Eddie step out. When she saw the goat, she said, "Now what in the name of peace are you bringing home?"

"It's just for the night, Katie," said Mr. Kilpatrick. "I'm helping my friend Eddie here."

"It's my goat, Mrs. Kilpatrick," said Eddie. "And Mr. Kilpatrick says I have to talk to Papa, so he won't give it to the Cruelty to Animals. Mr. Kilpatrick says I have to use— what kind of dip is it, Mr. Kilpatrick?"

"Diplomacy," said Mr. Kilpatrick.

"Diplomacy," said Eddie.

"Well!" said Mrs. Kilpatrick. "See that that goat is out of here tomorrow."

"It's all right, Katie," said Mr. Kilpatrick. "It's just for tonight."

Mr. Kilpatrick had a great big wooden box with a hinged lid. He turned it on its side and propped the lid open. "This will make a good house for a goat," he said. "I'll go over and get some straw from the livery stable and you won't have to worry about your goat. She'll be comfortable for the night."

"Thanks, Mr. Kilpatrick," said Eddie. "Any time you want me to keep anything of yours I'll be glad to. Any turtles or anything."

"That's O.K., Eddie," said Mr. Kilpatrick. "Just talk to your father tonight. I'll bring the goat over tomorrow after school."

Eddie patted his goat on the head and ran off with a light heart.

When Eddie reached home, he told his brothers about the goat. They thought it would be wonderful to have a goat. "But I don't think Dad will let us have it," said Rudy.

"Well, just leave it to me," said Eddie. "I'm going to use dip... Well, anyway, I'm going to use it."

At dinner that evening Eddie said, "Papa, you know that goat we had in school?"

"Goat?" said his father. "Oh, yes! What about it?"

"Well, it's an awful nice goat," said Eddie.

"They smell terrible," said Mr. Wilson.

"This one doesn't," said Eddie.

"Eddie," said his father, "if you are thinking of bringing that goat here, you can forget it right now."

"Oh, Papa!" Eddie groaned.

"I think it would be swell to have a goat," said Frank.

"We could harness it to the express wagon and it could pull the groceries home for Mother," said Joe.

Eddie beamed on Joe. He began to think that Joe was smarter than Rudy.

"Goats give milk," said Rudy. "Good milk."

Mr. Wilson looked at his four sons and said, *"No goat!"*

The next day when Mr. Kilpatrick's red car appeared in front of the Wilsons' house, Eddie ran out. "Here's your goat," said Mr. Kilpatrick. "Did you fix things up with your father?"

"Oh, Mr. Kilpatrick!" cried Eddie. "I have to use some more dip... What kind of dip did you say it is?"

"Diplomacy!" Mr. Kilpatrick shouted. "Diplomacy!"

"Well, I have to do it some more," said Eddie. "Will you keep the goat tonight?"

Mr. Kilpatrick did not look as though he were going to keep the goat for five more minutes until Eddie said, "Please, Mr. Kilpatrick, just tonight."

"O.K.!" said Mr. Kilpatrick, "but you have to take her tomorrow. Mrs. Kilpatrick won't stand for it. This goat ate all the flowers in the front garden and Mrs. Kilpatrick won't stand for it."

"Just tonight, Mr. Kilpatrick," said Eddie. "Just tonight. Please."

Mr. Kilpatrick drove off with the goat and that night at dinner Eddie said, "Papa, you know that goat we had at school?"

"Yes, Eddie," said his father. "What about the goat now?"

"Well, it's an awful nice goat," said Eddie.

"So you said before," said Mr. Wilson.

"A goat would eat the grass and we wouldn't have to cut it so often," said Joe.

Mr. Wilson looked around the table. "*No goat!*" he said. "Positively no goat!"

The following day was Saturday. After breakfast Eddie went over to Mr. Kilpatrick's to see his goat. As he walked up the path from the front gate, Mrs. Kilpatrick called out, "Eddie Wilson, you get that goat out of here! It ate up my flowers and this morning it ate up one of Mr. Kilpatrick's woolen socks. You take that goat home with you."

"Oh, Mrs. Kilpatrick!" said Eddie. "You'll just have to keep it for me one more night. I think my father likes the goat better every day and I think he will let me have it tomorrow."

"Well, if it eats up one more thing, out it goes," said Mrs. Kilpatrick.

At lunch Eddie said, "Papa, you know that goat?"

"Yes, Eddie," said his father.

"Well, it's an awful nice goat," said Eddie. Mr. Wilson looked at Eddie's mother and they both laughed. "O.K.!" said Eddie's father. "But let me tell you this. If it smells, out it goes."

Little Eddie's face broke into a wide grin.

"Hurrah!" cried the twins.

"Swell!" shouted Rudy.

"Where is the goat?" Mr. Wilson asked.

"It's over at Mr. Kilpatrick's. He's keeping it for me," said Eddie.

When lunch was over, Eddie and his three brothers went over to Mr. Kilpatrick's to get the goat. When they arrived, Eddie was carrying a package in his hand.

Mr. Kilpatrick opened the door. "Papa says we can have the goat," said Eddie, "but only if it doesn't smell."

"Well, it doesn't smell much," said Mr. Kilpatrick. "It's only billy goats that smell real bad."

"I can fix that," said Eddie, opening his package. "I bought some perfume at the Five and Ten. It's gardenia."

When the little goat saw Eddie, she ran to

meet him. "She knows me," Eddie cried, as he rubbed gardenia perfume all over the goat.

There was a great deal of excitement over getting the goat to the Wilsons' because Mr. Kilpatrick offered to give Eddie the big wooden box that had been the goat's house for the past two nights. It was too big to go into the trunk of Mr. Kilpatrick's car and for a while it looked as though the house could not be moved.

Then Eddie had an idea. "I know!" he cried. "Let's see if Mr. Ward will bring the fire engine over."

Mr. Kilpatrick telephoned to Mr. Ward, and about half an hour later Mr. Wilson saw the fire engine stop in front of his house. On the front seat sat Mr. Ward and Eddie with the goat between them and in the back were the other three boys with the big wooden box.

As Mr. Wilson helped the boys to carry the box to the back of the garage, he said, "Phew!"

"What's the matter?" said Eddie, looking frightened.

"I smell gardenia," said his father.

"Sure," said Eddie, with a wide grin, "that's my goat. Nice, isn't it, Papa?"

And so they named Eddie's little goat Gardenia.

Chapter Nine

Gardenia and the Pies

Gardenia grew rapidly and it was not long before she was a full-sized goat.

As soon as school closed for the summer vacation, Eddie and his brothers set to work building a wagon that Gardenia could pull. They used their old express wagon, and with their father's help they fastened a shaft to it. Gardenia did not seem too pleased with the idea of being put to work. She had been leading a very easy life, just eating and sleeping, and so it took a little time to get her to pull the wagon. But finally the day came when Gardenia pulled the wagon all the way around the block with Eddie sitting in it. Eddie was delighted.

The following day Eddie and the twins offered to go to the store for their mother and bring home the week's groceries. While they hitched up Gardenia to the wagon, Mrs. Wilson made out a long list. Joe put it in his pocket and the boys started off.

About a mile and a half from the Wilsons' house there was a great big market. It was so big that it was called a Supermarket. The boys always liked to go there because they like to help themselves to the things on the many shelves and put them in the wire basket which they could wheel up one aisle and down the other.

The boys took turns riding in the wagon all the way to the market. When they reached the big building, they found the street lined with trucks and automobiles, so Eddie took the goat and wagon around to the parking lot behind the market.

The twins went inside. Joe tore the shopping

list in half and gave the lower half to Frank. They each took a little cart with a wire basket and pushed it toward the places where the things on each list were kept.

Joe whizzed over to the freezer that held the frozen foods. He dug down and pulled up a package of lima beans. He liked to put his arm into the freezer. It made his arm feel cold and the cold air cooled his face. He was glad his mother wanted a lot of frozen foods.

Frank made his way along the shelves that contained cereals. "Oatmeal for Father," said Frank to himself. "Shredded wheat for Rudy, puffed wheat for Eddie, and rice crispies for me."

Mother was not fussy; she just ate whatever she picked up. Frank's basket was pretty full when he pushed it along to the shelf that held the soap powders. "Mother certainly put all the big things at the bottom of the list," thought Frank.

Eddie stood beside Gardenia on the parking lot and watched the baked goods being unloaded from a large truck. The driver carried one large tray after another into the store. There were iced cakes and plain cakes. There were cup cakes and cookies. There were cinnamon buns and coffee cakes, bread and rolls, tarts and pies. Tray after tray was moved from the truck into the store.

Suddenly Eddie heard a sound that always filled him with excitement. It was the sound of fire sirens and they were coming nearer. Eddie looked at Gardenia. She was quietly nibbling at a patch of grass that grew beside the parking lot.

Eddie ran around the building and out on the curb just in time to see the first of the fire engines swing into the main street. It rushed past, followed by the hook and ladder.

Joe and Frank had left their baskets inside the store and were standing beside Eddie. Everyone else had left their baskets, too. In fact, the store was empty. Even the driver of the bakery truck was out on the pavement, looking at the fire engines.

The three boys, forgetting all about Gardenia and their marketing, started to run after the fire engines. The driver of the bakery truck ran, too. He had such long legs and ran so fast that he was soon out of sight.

Meanwhile, Gardenia grew tired of eating grass. For some time she had been smelling a very delicious odor and now she moved toward it. Soon she was right up against the bakery truck. The delicious odor seemed to come from the back of the truck, so Gardenia made her way around to it. There she poked her nose inside the truck. She ran it along the edge of a large tray of pies. In a moment she had the tray between her teeth and it was easy to give it a jerk. *Wham* went the tray and at Gardenia's feet lay one dozen huckleberry pies, knocked very much out of shape. But Gardenia did not care about the shape of the pies. It was the flavor that interested her and the flavor of those huckleberry pies made Gardenia feel very happy indeed. Twelve pies were never eaten faster than Gardenia ate them. It was too bad she was not in a pie-eating contest, for she would certainly have won the prize. Soon there were smears of blueberries all over the ground behind the truck and there were blueberries all over Gardenia's face.

When she had finished most of the last pie, she went back for more. Again she stuck her head into the truck, ran her nose across another tray, clamped her teeth over the edge and pulled. There was a shower of pies and twelve more broke into pieces on the ground in front of Gardenia. These were cherry pies.

Out on the street the boys had run about three blocks when they saw the fire engines coming back. When the hose truck reached them, the boys called to the fireman, "Where was the fire?" The firemen waved to them and called back, "False alarm!" Riding on the back of the hose truck was the bakery man.

Gardenia was in the midst of eating up the cherry pies when the driver of the bakery truck appeared. When he saw Gardenia, he let out such a yell that Gardenia galloped off, pulling

the express wagon after her. She ran out of the parking lot, past the market, and lickety-split up the street, with the bakery man after her.

Eddie and the twins were walking toward the market. They had forgotten all about Gardenia, but when Eddie saw Gardenia coming head on, he shouted, "Geepers! Here comes Gardenia! I forgot all about her!"

The boys ran toward her, but Gardenia rushed right past them with a great clatter. The bakery man rushed past them, too. Eddie and the twins joined the chase and they all went pell-mell up the street after Gardenia.

At the next corner, in order to clear a parked car, Gardenia ran up on the pavement, knocking the wagon against a fire plug. Off went one of the wheels, which rolled like a hoop down the street toward the boys. Frank caught it while Eddie and Joe ran on.

Now that the wagon had only three wheels, it was harder for Gardenia to pull it, so she had to slow down. Presently she stopped and began nibbling at the grass on the edge of the lawn.

The bakery man stopped, too, and took hold of Gardenia's harness. By this time Eddie and Joe had reached the goat and Frank was coming up with the wagon wheel.

"Whose goat is this anyway?" said the bakery man.

"She's mine," said Eddie.

"Well, you come along with me," said the man. "Just wait until you see what this goat did!"

At this moment Eddie saw Gardenia's face. "Oh! Oh!" he cried. "Look at her! Look at her! She's done something to her face. She's hurt herself! Oh, Gardenia!" he cried, kneeling down beside his goat. "Look at the blood all over her face. Look! Red blood! And oh look! Blue blood!"

"Blue blood, my eye!" shouted the bakery man. "Huckleberry pie, that is! My huckleberry and cherry pies!"

"It is?" said Eddie, sitting back on his heels and looking up at the man.

"It certainly is!" said the man "And you're

going to have to pay for them. You just come along with me."

Joe unharnessed Gardenia and they all started back for the market. Eddie had to pull Gardenia. She didn't seem anxious to return to the mess she had made of the pies. Joe followed with the remains of the wagon and Frank carried the wheel.

"Did she eat very many pies?" Eddie asked, looking up at the bakery man.

"I don't know how many she ate, but she ate plenty," said the man.

"Oh, that's too bad," said Eddie.

"It's going to be more than too bad," he replied. "It's going to be plenty bad."

When they reached the market, the bakery man, Eddie, the twins, and the goat marched back to the parking lot.

"Just look at that!" cried the man, pointing to the ground where cherries and blueberries and broken pieces of pie still lay.

"Oh, that's too bad!" said Eddie.

"Stop saying it's too bad!" said the man. "I'll

soon tell you how bad it is." And he looked at the shelves in the back of the truck. Someone had picked up the trays that had held the pies and put them back on the rack.

"Two trays!" cried the man.

"Two trays?" Eddie repeated.

"Two trays is right! That's twenty-four pies," said the bakery man.

"Twenty-four pies!" gasped Eddie. "Geepers! That's an awful lot of pie! Did Gardenia eat all of 'em?"

"All but those two on the ground," said the man. "And she might as well've ate them. They're no good to me."

"Geepers!" said Eddie. "That sure is too bad."

"You mean it's twenty-two bad and too bad the other two are busted on the ground," said the man. "Let's see. That's twenty-four pies at seventy cents apiece. That's sixteen dollars and eighty cents. That lunch your goat just ate will cost you exactly sixteen dollars and eighty cents."

Eddie could not believe his ears. Sixteen dollars and eighty cents! He looked at his brothers, who were standing by. They looked very solemn.

"Gee!" said Joe. "That's more than Mother gave us to do the marketing. She gave me a ten-dollar bill." Joe dug into his pocket and pulled out the ten-dollar bill.

"Well, hand over the ten-dollar bill and give me your name and address. I'll stop around later and collect the sixty-eighty," said the bakery man.

"O.K.!" said Joe sadly, as he handed the ten-dollar bill to the man. The man wrote their name and address in a little book.

The three boys walked home with the goat without saying a word. When they reached the house, they put the goat in her house, stood the wagon in the garage, and went indoors.

Mrs. Wilson was in the living room, hanging curtains. "Well!" she called out. "Did you get everything?"

Joe looked at Frank and Frank looked at

Eddie. Eddie gulped.

"You tell her," said Frank, giving Eddie a poke.

Eddie gulped again. Then he said, "We couldn't."

"Why not?" his mother asked.

"The wheel came off the wagon," said Eddie.

"Oh, that's too bad." said Mrs. Wilson.

"The bakery man said it was twenty-two bad," said Frank.

"Twenty-two what?" asked his mother.

"Twenty-two pies," said Frank.

"I didn't tell you to get twenty-two pies," said Mrs. Wilson.

"We didn't," said Joe.

"What are you talking about?" said Mrs. Wilson, sitting down.

"Gardenia," said Eddie.

"Well, what about Gardenia?" his mother asked.

"She ate some pie," said Eddie.

"Oh!" said Mrs. Wilson. "How much pie did Gardenia eat?"

"Well," said Eddie, "she didn't eat all of it. Did she?" he asked, turning to the twins.

"No," said Joe, and Frank added, "Not all."

"Well, how much did she eat?" Mrs. Wilson asked.

"She ate all but two," said Eddie.

"*All but two!*" said his mother. "Just how many pies did Gardenia eat?"

Eddie swallowed very hard and said, "Only twenty-two."

"*Twenty-two!*" cried Mrs. Wilson. "Gardenia ate twenty-two pies? And where were you while Gardenia was eating twenty-two pies?"

The three boys hung their heads. "Running after the fire engines," said Eddie.

"I might have known there would be a fire engine in this," said Mrs. Wilson. "It seems to me that no matter what you do, Eddie, you always get mixed up with a fire engine." Then she added, "I suppose you paid for the pies?"

"We didn't have enough money," said Frank. "It came to sixteen dollars and eighty cents. We gave the man the ten-dollar bill and he took our name and address. He said he would come over and collect it."

Mrs. Wilson shook her head. "Sixteen dollars and eighty cents!" she said. "Sixteen dollars and eighty cents for pies for a goat! Wait until your father hears about this! I know one thing. We are going to get rid of that goat."

The three boys sat on three chairs, looking very unhappy.

Suddenly Mrs. Wilson had an idea. She looked at the three boys and said, "Where was the bakery man while Gardenia was eating all those pies?"

Before the boys had a chance to answer the question, the doorbell rang and Mrs. Wilson got up and went to the door.

The boys looked out of the window and saw the bakery truck.

Very quietly they all tiptoed upstairs.

"Well," said Mrs. Wilson when she opened the door, "I hear our goat had quite a pie feast and that you have come to collect six dollars and eighty cents."

"No," said the bakery man. "My boss told me to stop over and give you back your ten dollars. He said I shouldn't have left the truck."

"Where were you?" asked Mrs. Wilson.

The bakery man turned bright pink and looked very sheepish. "Well," he said, "ever since I was a boy I've been crazy about fire engines. Can't leave 'em alone. Just let me hear a fire siren and I gotta run."

"I hope you aren't going to lose your job because of this," said Mrs. Wilson.

"No, the boss says he'll give me another chance," said the man. "But he says if it happens again I better join the fire department."

Mrs. Wilson laughed. "Your name ought to be Eddie."

"Matter of fact, it is," said the bakery man. "Eddie Murphy. That's me."

Chapter Ten

The September Fair Comes Again

When Mr. Wilson heard about Gardenia and the pies he said it was time to get rid of Gardenia.

"But the pies didn't cost us anything," said Eddie.

"Gardenia is a great nuisance," said his father, "and good for nothing. This is no place for a goat, anyway. She should be out on a farm."

"O.K., Papa!" said Eddie. "What shall we do with her?"

"Oh, give her to Mr. Kilpatrick or Mr. Ward

or the firemen," said Mr. Wilson. "I don't care who you give her to, but give her to somebody. And do it today."

"O.K., Papa!" said Eddie.

On his way to school Eddie stopped to speak to Mr. Kilpatrick. "Mr. Kilpatrick," said Eddie, "would you like to have my goat, Gardenia?"

"So you're going to give her away!" said Mr. Kilpatrick. "Well, Eddie, it was nice of you to think of me and I appreciate it, but you know how Mrs. Kilpatrick feels about that goat. She'd put me out of the house if I brought that goat home again."

"O.K.," said Eddie.

After school he got on the bus and went over to Mr. Ward's used car lot. He found Mr. Ward putting a new battery in a car.

"Hello, Mr. Ward!" said Eddie.

"How you doin', Eddie?" said Mr. Ward.

"Fine," said Eddie. "Mr. Ward, would you like to have Gardenia?"

"Who's Gardenia?" said Mr. Ward.

"My goat," said Eddie.

"That goat that ate up the pies?" cried Mr. Ward. "No, thanks."

"How's the fire engine running?" Eddie asked.

"It's in good shape," said Mr. Ward. "But I have to get rid of it. I need the space on the lot."

Mr. Ward stood up and wiped his hands. "Do you know what I'm planning to do?" he said.

"What?" said Eddie.

"I'm going to donate that fire engine to the September Fair and they're going to auction it off to the highest bidder," said Mr. Ward.

"What do you mean, auction it off?" asked Eddie, looking puzzled.

"It will be sold to the person who offers the most money for it," replied Mr. Ward.

"Geepers!" cried Eddie. "Do you think I could buy it? How much money do you think I'd need to get it?"

"I don't know," said Mr. Ward. "You never can tell about auctions."

"Do you think more than ten dollars?" said Eddie. "I've got ten dollars saved up in my bank."

"Oh! They'll get a great deal more than ten dollars for it," said Mr. Ward. "I figure they ought to get at least a hundred for it."

Eddie's face suddenly grew long. "A hundred dollars!" he said. "Oh, I could never pay that much. I never had a hundred dollars. Not in my whole life."

"Well, I'll tell you what!" said Mr. Ward. "Why don't you sell that goat of yours instead of giving it away? You could make some money that way."

"Do you think I could auction Gardenia?" asked Eddie.

"That's a good idea," said Mr. Ward. "Sell Gardenia at auction and use the money to buy the fire engine."

"I sure am glad I came to see you, Mr. Ward," said Eddie. "How do I do this auction business?"

"Well," said Mr. Ward, "first you have to

make a big sign that says *Auction Sale!* Then the day—*Wednesday*, we'll say. *One Fine Goat. Name—Gardenia!*"

"Oh, I can make a good sign," said Eddie. "I like to make signs. What else should the sign say?"

"Just where the auction is going to be held, that's all," Mr. Ward replied.

"Where do you think I should have the sale?" Eddie asked.

"It ought to be some place convenient," said Mr. Ward. "The ball grounds back of the firehouse would be good."

"That would be swell," said Eddie. "Then what do I do?"

"Well, first you get a soap box," said Mr. Ward, "and you stand back of the soap box with a hammer in your hand and you point to the goat and you say, 'What am I offered for this very fine and elegant goat?' And somebody calls out, 'Twenty-five dollars.' And you say, 'Twenty-five dollars! Do I hear thirty?' And somebody calls out, 'Thirty dollars!' And you say, 'Thirty dollars! Do I hear thirty-five?' And you go on until somebody says, 'One hundred dollars.' Then you say, 'One hundred dollars! One hundred dollars once! One hundred dollars twice!' And then when you say one hundred dollars the third time, you bring the hammer down on the soap box and you call out, 'Sold! For one hundred dollars!'"

"Gee! That's super!" said Eddie. "Then I'll have a hundred dollars to pay for the fire engine."

Eddie went home and spent the rest of the day painting a sign. It said:

OCSHUN SALE
SATURDaY SEPTEMBer 5th
VERY ELEGANT GoAT To Be
SoLD ON B ALL FIELD BACK of
FI RE HOUSE AT 1 0 CLock

The firemen let Eddie tack the sign to the wall of the firehouse.

When the day came, a large crowd gathered behind the firehouse by one o'clock, for the ball game was at two. Now that the time had come for Eddie to part with Gardenia, he felt very unhappy. In fact, he could hardly swallow because of the lump in his throat. He had to keep thinking of how much he wanted the fire engine in order to sell Gardenia. Joe held Gardenia by the collar that she was wearing, while Eddie placed his soap box in front of the crowd. They were mostly boys, but the firemen had come, too.

Eddie raised his hammer and called out, "How much does somebody give for this very nice goat?"

There was not a sound from anyone. So Eddie said again, "How much does somebody give for this nice goat? She's the nicest goat in the world."

Then someone called out, "Twenty-five cents."

Eddie looked very much surprised. "Twenty-five cents, did you say?"

"Twenty-five cents!" came the voice.

Eddie said, "Twenty-five cents. Do I hear thirty?"

Eddie did not hear thirty. So he repeated the question.

There was silence.

Then Eddie said, "Somebody's supposed to say thirty."

A deep voice rang out. "Thirty cents!"

Eddie looked relieved. He said, "Thirty cents! Do I heart thirty-five?"

He did not hear thirty-five.

"Do I hear thirty-five?" said Eddie.

He did not.

"Isn't anybody going to say thirty-five?" said Eddie.

"Guess not," Billy Porter called out.

Eddie looked around and saw Mr. Ward in the back of the crowd of boys. "What do I do now, Mr. Ward?" he called out. "Nobody will say a hundred dollars. They won't even say thirty-five cents."

"Well, Eddie, you have to sell her to the

highest bidder," Mr. Ward replied.

"Do I say, 'thirty cents once'?" Eddie asked.

"That's right," said Mr. Ward.

So Eddie raised his hammer and called out, "Thirty cents once! Thirty cents twice!" Then he banged the hammer on the soap box and called out, "Sold for thirty cents!"

To Eddie's surprise, one of the firemen stepped forward and handed him the thirty cents. "She'll be a good mascot for the fire department," said the fireman.

There had been tears in Eddie's eyes, but now he said, "Oh that's swell! Then I can come and see her, can't I?"

"Oh sure!" the fireman said.

By the time the day arrived for the September Fair, Eddie had exactly twelve dollars and thirty cents. He hoped with all his heart that no one would have more than twelve dollars and thirty cents to spend for the fire engine, for he had persuaded his father to let him keep the fire engine, if he got it, on an empty plot of ground beside the garage.

"What are you going to do with it if you get it?" asked his father. "You can't run it. You're not old enough. Even Rudy isn't old enough."

Eddie looked up at his father and smiled his wide smile. "You'll run it for me, won't you, Papa? We can go for rides."

It was then that Mr. Wilson had said that Eddie could have it. "But," added Mr. Wilson, "I don't think you'll get it. They'll be able to sell it for more than twelve dollars and thirty cents."

The day of the Fair was a beautiful fall day. Eddie went over to the fair grounds early in the morning for he did not want to miss anything. The booths were being decorated and signs were being tacked up. Cars were driving into the grounds and were being unloaded. Eddie thought it was a little like watching a parade, as people passed carrying cakes and candy and pies and dolls and toys, and boxes of all sizes and shapes.

Soon the ice-cream truck drove up and unloaded a case containing ice cream and a whole stack of great big cans filled with cones.

Then the loud-speaker truck arrived just before Eddie's mother drove in with Rudy and the twins. Eddie ran to the car and opened the door.

"Everything's going fine," he said. "But the fire engine isn't here yet."

"Eddie, please help us carry some of these sandwiches," said his mother, handing him a large platter piled high with sandwiches wrapped in wax paper.

Eddie now joined the parade with the platter of sandwiches.

About eleven o'clock Eddie heard the siren and bell of the fire engine and in a moment he saw it swing into the fair grounds. All the children who had been waiting for it to arrive shouted, and the firemen waved to them.

Eddie was the first one to climb on. In less than a minute the fire engine was filled with children and it was off for its first trip. When it returned there was a long line of children waiting to climb aboard for the next trip. Eddie rode on the fire engine only once, because he was saving his money to buy it.

At four o'clock Mr. Ward announced over the loud speaker that the fire engine was about to be sold at auction. "All those interested in the sale will please gather round the fire engine."

Eddie didn't have to gather round. He was already there. In a few minutes there was a big crowd.

Mr. Ward stood up in the back of the fire engine with a croquet mallet in his hand. He rapped it on the brass railing of the fire engine. The crowd grew quiet. Then he called out, "What am I bid for this magnificent genuine fire engine?"

"Twelve dollars and thirty cents!" Eddie shouted.

"Twelve dollars and thirty cents!" Mr. Ward repeated. "Do I hear fifteen dollars?"

A big voice boomed out, "Fifteen dollars!"

Eddie's heart sank, for he couldn't bid any more. He heard Mr. Ward say, "Fifteen dollars! Do I hear twenty?"

There was not a sound from anyone, but Mr. Ward saw someone way in the back of the crowd hold up his hand. Mr. Ward called out, "Twenty dollars! Do I hear twenty-five?"

"But Mr. Ward," said Eddie, "you didn't hear twenty dollars."

Mr. Ward looked down at Eddie and said, "A gentleman in the rear raised his hand. That means he'll pay twenty dollars."

"Oh!" said Eddie, looking as though he were going to cry.

"Do I hear twenty-five?" Mr. Ward called out.

There was silence.

Mr. Ward waited and then he said, "Ladies and gentlemen, do you mean to tell me that no one is willing to pay more than twenty dollars for this magnificent fire engine? Why, the bell alone is worth twenty dollars!"

There wasn't a peep out of anyone, so finally Mr. Ward raised his mallet and called out, "Twenty dollars once! Twenty dollars twice! Sold for twenty dollars to the gentleman in the rear!" And he brought down his mallet.

Eddie was too little to see who the gentleman was and he was too unhappy to care. He just ran home. When he reached his own room, he locked the door, threw himself on his bed, and cried. He had wanted that fire engine more than he had ever wanted anything in his whole life. And now he did not even know where it was going. But he did not care much, because what difference did it make if it was not his own? He wished he had Gardenia back. He wished he had never sold her.

Eddie cried until he fell asleep. He woke up when the family came home from the Fair for dinner. He could hear them talking downstairs. Then he heard a tap on his door and his mother's voice. "Eddie," she said, "open the door for Mother."

Eddie got up and opened the door. When his mother saw his sad, tear-stained face, she threw her arms around him and said, "Don't be unhappy about the fire engine, darling."

"But I wanted it so badly," said Eddie, with a

sob in his voice. "I really wanted it very badly, Mama."

"Well, darling, we all want things sometimes that we don't get," said his mother. "Sometimes we have to wait for them and sometimes something much nicer comes instead."

"There couldn't be anything nicer than the fire engine," said Eddie. "Who bought it?"

"Some gentleman," replied Mrs. Wilson.

"I don't want any supper," said Eddie.

"Well, how would you like to get into bed, and I'll bring you some soup on a tray?" his mother asked.

Eddie looked cheered for the first time. "You will?" he said.

"Yes," replied Mrs. Wilson. "And some dessert?"

"What you got?" Eddie asked.

"Apple pie," replied his mother.

"I guess I could eat a little apple pie," said Eddie.

"How about a little roast chicken?" said his mother.

"Oh, I guess a little," said Eddie.

"No vegetables?" said his mother.

"Well, I guess a few vegetables," said Eddie.

"Very well," said Mrs. Wilson. "You get undressed and hop into bed. Don't forget to wash."

As Mrs. Wilson was going downstairs, Eddie called, "Mama, don't forget the salad and the rolls, and Mama, can I have a piece of cheese with the apple pie?"

Eddie had been so excited about the Fair and the fire engine that he had almost forgotten that the following day was his birthday. When he woke up very early on Sunday morning, he went to his window and looked out. He thought he must still be asleep. He must be having a wonderful dream! It was too good to be true. He rubbed his eyes and looked again. But it really was true. There in the driveway of his own house stood the fire engine! Leaning against the brass rail was a great big sign. It said "Happy Birthday to Eddie from Papa."

Eddie rushed into his father's room and

jumped into his bed. "Oh, Papa!" he cried. "Oh, Papa! It's mine! It's mine! Did you buy it, Papa?"

"Yes, I bought it," said his father.

"Were you the man who held up his hand when Mr. Ward said, 'Do I hear twenty'?"

"I was the man," said his father. "Now let me go to sleep."

"Oh, thank you, Papa! Thank you!" said Eddie.

Two hours later, when Mr. Wilson got up, he looked out the window in the hall, and there was Eddie proudly sitting at the wheel of the fire engine. But something else was on the fire engine too.

"Jumping grasshoppers!" exclaimed Eddie's father. "Is that Gardenia on the fire engine?"

"That," replied Eddie's mother, "is Gardenia. The firemen gave her to Eddie for his birthday. I believe she ate the pies they bought at the Fair."